Ros wanted something more

She wanted the magic ingredient to lift her relationship with Alan out of the comfortably ordinary into the special, champagne class. Perhaps she wanted too much.

What she most certainly didn't want was to find Dan Maxton in the courtyard of the Stables looking like trouble, even in an Italian suit.

"Where have you been all day?" he asked aggressively. "This is the third time I've called."

The tension screaming in Ros for release came out in a rush.

"Mr. Maxton," she snapped. "It may interest you to know that there was a life before you. My life goes on in spite of your eruption into it. And it will go on more sweetly once you've taken yourself off— which you could start doing right now!"

Alison York is a welcome contributor to the Harlequin Romance line. The fast-paced style of her writing and lively, well-developed characters have become popular with readers.

Books by Alison York

HARLEQUIN ROMANCE
2880—NO SAD SONG
2970—THAT DEAR PERFECTION

Don't miss any of our special offers. Write to us at the following address for information on our newest releases

Harlequin Reader Service
901 Fuhrmann Blvd., P.O. Box 1397, Buffalo, NY 14240
Canadian address: P.O. Box 603,
Fort Erie, Ont. L2A 5X3

The Maxton Bequest

Alison York

Harlequin Books

TORONTO • NEW YORK • LONDON
AMSTERDAM • PARIS • SYDNEY • HAMBURG
STOCKHOLM • ATHENS • TOKYO • MILAN

Original hardcover edition published in 1989
by Mills & Boon Limited

ISBN 0-373-03042-8

Harlequin Romance first edition March 1990

CHAPTER ONE

ROS WAS perched precariously on a stepladder, reaching for the branch Tammy was holding up for her to fix over the last stable door to be decorated, when she saw him for the first time.

Perhaps she noticed him in particular among all the people milling around in the courtyard because he was standing quite still in the gateway, only his incredibly dark eyes moving as he watched the preparations for the Midsummer's Eve party. Or maybe it was his clothes that drew her attention. Certainly the soft grey leather of his jacket and the elegant fit of the black polo-necked sweater and dark trousers were well above the scruffy casuals the others were wearing. It could simply have been that, even if you discounted the clothes, he was just the sort of man who got himself noticed anywhere . . . tall, cool and authoritative, carrying every inch of his rangy frame with easy pride.

Ros snapped out of her momentary trance and turned back to the branch.

'Is he one of yours?' she asked Tammy, giving a brief nod of her fair head in the appropriate direction.

Tammy looked, and raised her sandy eyebrows in instant approval. 'No. But he could be if he fancied it. Paul must have invited him. Not that he looks like

5

one of Paul's usuals.'

'Maybe he's a customer. He looks as though he could buy most things he wants.'

Fixing the branch demanded the concentration of both of them for the next few minutes, and called for a dodgy collaboration on the ladder. When they had finished, Ros left Tammy to put the steps away and threaded a risky path through the kids from Gateway towards the stranger, dodging rogue wheelchairs with the skill of familiarity.

The top of her head was just about level with his shoulders—and she wasn't small, and now that she was close she could see that his eyes were such a dark, velvety brown that it was hard to tell where pupil ended and iris began. Confusing eyes, they were. Eyes that were difficult to read.

'You must be one of Paul's guests, we've decided,' she said, smiling a welcome.

He pushed briefly before replying. 'Paul . . . yes. And could you be Roslyn Howard?'

'That's me—but I usually get called just Ros. I'm afraid Paul didn't tell us your name.'

'Dan. They abbreviate me, too,' he said with a straight face.

And I bet that's the only way they cut you down, Ros thought, noticing the tough line of his jaw and suppressing a wince at the strength of his grip on the hand she had so innocently offered.

'I gather Paul's going to be late?' he went on.

'Half an hour or so. The gallery that shows his stuff wanted his latest wood-carving for someone to see this evening, and he didn't finish fiddling with it until the last minute. You know Paul!'

He was watching Tammy stagger out to the trestle table with a tray loaded with flans and salads.

'Is all this in honour of Midsummer's Eve?'

'Midsummer's Eve by chance, really. It happened that we moved in here three years ago on that particular day, so it's a sort of anniversary for Tammy and Paul and me.' Ros dodged as a wheelchair came a bit too close. 'This is the first time we've had my kids from Gateway here.'

'Your kids?' One heavy dark eyebrow rose quizzically.

'Mine in the sense that I teach them. They're a bit over-excited at the moment. They're not usually such bad drivers!'

'The one over by the table doesn't look too happy.'

Ros knew without following his gaze which of the children he was talking about. She moved slightly so that her back was towards the little brown-haired, pale-faced girl sitting so rigidly in her chair, cut off from the obvious enjoyment of the rest as thoroughly as though a glass screen surrounded her. It wouldn't do for Debra to think she was being talked about.

'That's Debra. It isn't long since her accident. She hasn't adjusted yet, but she will. She's got plenty of courage, once she finds the right way to use it. Just now she's wasting it on being rebellious. I'm hoping the dancing will bring her out of herself.'

'Dancing?' He was looking at her as though she was mad. 'Forgive my obtuseness—but how can watching people dance do anything for someone in a wheelchair? Surely it's only going to drive home the rottenness of her own situation?'

'You can't have heard of the Wheelchair Olympics.' Ros smiled patiently. 'When I say "dance" I mean everyone joins in, whether they're on legs or wheels. People don't lose a sense of rhythm, you know, just because they can't exploit it in the same way. You'll see, once we get going.'

'Amateur psychiatrists are on pretty dangerous ground, it's always seemed to me,' he said, those inscrutable eyes looking steadily at her.

'If you call "amateur psychiatry" the result of a year's specialised training at the end of my course, then three years working steadily at Gateway, then nothing I can tell you will convince you,' Ros told him calmly. 'But I'd say that the end of the evening would be a better time to form your judgement.'

He didn't get a chance to reply. At that moment, Alan Scott, the head of Gateway, called to her across the courtyard.

'Any chance of getting going, Ros? They'll do themselves an injury if we don't harness all this energy soon.'

'Coming!' she shouted back, then turned to the stranger again. 'Don't go away. I shall be expecting a U-turn from you later.'

'Will you?' She suddenly realised that there had been pale laughter-lines at the corners of his eyes, lost now in the attractive crinkles of bronzed skin formed by his lazy smile. 'And if you don't get one?'

'Then I shall either be wrong, which I don't anticipate, or you'll be an MCP of the first order, which doesn't sound like a friend of Paul's. See you later.'

Her long peasant skirt swirled out in a defiant rainbow of bright colours as she turned and ran lightly over towards the audio system they had brought out into the yard.

'Saving your energy for dancing?' she said to Debra as she passed. 'You're very wise.'

'What energy?' Debra said with a cynicism no ten-year-old ought to have.

'Wait until the music starts. You'll surprise yourself,' Ros told her as she ducked under the extension flex coming from the house which formed the end of the courtyard opposite the gate. She wished she felt as confident as she sounded. There was every possibility that Debra wouldn't join in with the others, judging by her track record so far, and that would give this Dan fellow every chance to crow. And if he does—what the hell does it matter? It's what Debra does that counts, she told herself impatiently, running a quick eye over the food laid out on the trestles under cling-film, then checking that the barn dance record was on the turntable before clapping her hands to draw attention.

'Right, everybody,' she called when order of sorts was established. 'Let's get going! Take a partner and form a circle, legs inside facing out, wheels outside facing clockwise.'

There was a buzz of movement but, predictably, not from Debra. Dan had moved over, Ros noticed, probably to get within gloating distance.

'Look—here's a partner coming for you, Debra!'

she said, not entirely without malice towards the dark stranger.

'He needn't bother. I'm not doing it.' The child's face was mutinous.

'Nor me. I think it's a crazy idea.' Dan's wink was just quick enough to be over before Debra's head spun round to see who was the other sceptic. She looked back uncertainly at Ros to check her reaction, and Dan went on, 'I mean—who wants to have a wheelchair run over his foot? I certainly don't.'

'We're not stupid. We wouldn't roll all over your feet . . . not if we wanted to do the silly dance,' Debra said, realising rather late the trap she had almost fallen into.

'I'd rather not give you the chance. Sorry and all that. Nothing personal. I'm happy to wait it out with you.' He smiled pleasantly and settled back against the wall, hands in pockets.

'Come on over there! You're holding us up,' Tammy called from the middle of the circle.

'I'm afraid I haven't a partner,' Dan said with smooth hypocrisy.

'He doesn't want to, and neither do I,' Debra corrected.

'Personally,' Ros addressed both of them, 'I think anyone who writes off anything without giving it a go is a bit of a wally. If you do it and then decide it's not for you, fair enough. But you should at least give it a chance.'

There was a little silence. In the folds of her skirt, Ros crossed her fingers. Debra sneaked a look at Dan.

'I don't know . . .' he said uncertainly. 'I don't particularly like being called a wally. But can you really manage that chair?'

''Course I can!' Debra rolled forward and then back and turned in a circle. She shot a very feminine glance over her shoulder at him. 'It's easy.'

'Hey! That wasn't bad.' He looked again towards the circle, then back at Debra, and seemed to make up his mind. 'Well—I will if you will. Just once, not to be a wally. OK?'

'I suppose so.' She sighed and manoeuvred her chair into the outer circle, studiously not looking at Dan as he strolled past to the inner one.

There goes a man who knows how to get what he wants . . . Ros thought admiringly as she held the stylus over the first track on the record and began to run through the adapted instructions for the dance she and Tammy had carefully worked out. After one or two hiccups and a lot of laughter, children and adults got the hang of it and they got going to the music.

In the intervals when Tammy took over the calling, Ros was able to watch Dan and Debra go on from one dance to the next . . . and the next. Debra's initial reluctance gradually gave way to the real enjoyment Ros had hoped to see the child experience and, reassured, she found herself concentrating more on Dan's dark figure as he swung the wheelchair or promenaded alongside it, laughing down at the little girl he was partnering. There was no doubt that he was a prestige partner, and Debra realised it. He stood out from the rest, not just because of his build, but because he had an innate sense of rhythm that made his walk a swagger, each turn a flourish, and his whole attitude to his little partner not the enthusiastic good-natured blundering of the rest, but a kind of syncopated courtship. No wonder Debra responded so well. He was charming the hide off her!

Four dances on the trot were enough to tire both legs and arms, and a long supper break began.

Dan, who had been talking to Alan, waited until Ros had finished making sure with Tammy that everyone had a loaded plate before strolling over to her. The bonfire had caught well, and the flickering flames put a sheen on the crisp darkness of his hair and danced in twin miniatures in his eyes.

'Well?' she greeted him mischievously, her blonde head on one side.

'Very well! You were right, of course. You see before you something of a U-turn. I'm eating my words as well as your excellent food.'

'I suppose I must give you some credit for the smoothest bit of manipulation of the young female psyche I've ever watched,' Ros conceded.

'Who could help it? She's a great kid, and you were right about the guts. As we started, she rolled close enough to give my toes a bit of a nip, then said, "That's what I could do if I wanted. I shan't do it again"—and she didn't.' He saw that Ros had no plate. 'What about food for the hostess? Hold this for me and I'll collect some.'

She watched him move along the table, thinking again that he w s as far removed from Paul and his usual cronies as anyone could be. Paul wouldn't have noticed that she wasn't eating—and he'd be smelling of sawdust, not something spicy and expensive that she couldn't identify but rather liked. This man was surely a customer rather than a friend. It was odd that nothing had been said about him.

'Paul's not back yet,' she said as she thanked him for her plate.

He shot out his left arm and looked at the steel-grey watch on his wrist. 'No—and I'll have to be off any minute, I'm afraid. I was going to ask to see the workshops. You wouldn't like to show me around while everyone's occupied?'

'Gladly. You know Paul's work, so we could skip that.'

'Only some of it. I'd like to see everywhere.'

'Come on, then. We can eat as we go.'

'Just a minute.' He picked a buddleia flower out of her hair. 'Your decorations are clinging to you. Is there any special significance in the boughs over the doors?'

'It's a left-over from ancient village customs at this time of year.'

'One of the less earthy village customs?'

She grinned. 'We don't go in for the other sort.'

'But your headmaster rather looks as though he'd like to . . . with you, as it happens.'

Ros was taken aback. Alan was keen on her, she knew, but she hadn't realised it was obvious to others. Even the kids—never slow to air their shrewd observations—hadn't done any teasing yet. But this unknown quantity of a man had picked up the vibes she wasn't sure she wanted to come her way. She didn't respond to his remark.

'This is Paul's place,' she said, opening the first door for him to pass inside before closing it behind them and switching on the lights.

Dan walked about, looking with apparent interest at the few pieces still lying around in the workshop—rough, tiny woodland creatures that Paul's stubby, square fingers had conjured out of solid wood with such skill.

'These are the things he's been doing for the fête at Gateway,' she said. 'Money-raisers. Most of his larger pieces go straight to the gallery.'

'Like the fox he had to take this evening? These are good, though.' He looked at the circular saw and the turning equipment. 'Not the sort of machinery you could put in the average semi-detached house, is it? This place is ideal for you, I suppose. You say you've been here three years. How did you manage to find such a property?'

'By chance—complete chance.'

'Tell me.'

His unfathomable eyes were on her, and Ros picked up a gleaming wooden doormouse to give herself something to look at. There was an intensity about him that she found a bit disconcerting now that she was alone with him.

'It's not too long a story. I like walking, and I was following a public right of way through the woods skirting the Dower House—that's the big old Elizabethan property these stables belong to. I came across Max—Mr Maxton who owns the house, that is, and as he was obviously not at all well I stayed with him until the pill he'd managed to find in one of his pockets worked. He had angina, you see, and I suppose he shouldn't have been walking so far. I helped him back to the house and he wouldn't let me call a doctor—said it wasn't necessary. But as we sat talking I saw that he was really terrified of being shunted off into a home.' She flashed a quick look at the man listening so intently without comment. 'Max was a bit of an eccentric, you know. He couldn't keep housekeepers, and he seemed to have run through all the available local help at a rate of knots. The long and short of it was that I was scared he was going to bring on another attack as he told me about his problems. He was getting all worked up again. So I babbled on myself about my painting and about Paul and Tammy and their work, and about how difficult it was to find places where we could spread our clutter. He suddenly said he had stables and a house in the grounds, and he thought they'd be the right sort of place for us. I laughed, and said they'd be too grand for our pockets by far. Then he said, ''You seem the sort of girl I could get along with. You look after me, and I'll let you have the Stables at a peppercorn rent.'' '

'Look after him?'

Ros caught the flash of momentary suspicion in his eyes and flushed. She pushed her hair back impatiently.

'All three of us—and look after him literally, as in make meals, clean the two or three rooms he used—

see he was all right in the mornings and comfortable at nights. He was a very lonely, very vulnerable old man.'

'And it worked?'

'Very well indeed. We drew up a rota and we all grew very fond of Max. He was a great character. And the Stables are ideal for us, as you can see.'

'So the fairy-tale had a happy ending. Beauty met the Beast—who turned out to be a Fairy Godfather in disguise—and moved into the magic castle.'

'Not quite a fairy-story,' Ros said, feeling her blue eyes prick with the threat of tears. 'You see, Max died last week . . . in his own garden, actually, as he would have wished to do. But there's not going to be any "happy ever after" for us. We shall have to move out of the Stables soon, I expect. It's only a matter of time. I think this will be our last Midsummer's Eve party here.'

'I see.' He seemed at a loss what to say. Probably he was embarrassed by her threatened display of emotion. Ros moved briskly to the door, wishing she hadn't been so forthcoming. He was an absolute stranger, after all.

'We'd better move on if you want to see the other two workshops,' she said.

Tammy's place, spilling over with fabrics and trimmings, didn't interest him much, though he did comment briefly on the delicate stitchery that went into her cushions. Ros suppressed a smile as he turned the creation of silk and ribbon and lace over in his strong fingers. He was such a man's man, and Tammy's cushions were so very feminine.

They moved quickly on to the stable nearest the house, Ros's own workshop, with the cool smell of clay and paint hitting them as soon as she opened the door.

He picked up and examined several of the 'Woodland' series dishes she had done for the Gateway fête, and seemed to approve of the delicate wild flowers and fruits of the forest decorations, but it was the Avon miniatures that he really seemed to like best.

'You've got quite a thing for this river, haven't you?' he said.

'For water of any kind. I think it's the part of nature that fascinates me most. All the reflections . . . and the darkness underneath.' She had a sudden quick recollection, conjured up by her own words, of the twin bonfires flickering in those inscrutable eyes of his. There was certainly darkness underneath there.

'Ros!' Young voices were calling impatiently from the yard.

'It sounds as though the interlude's over,' Dan said. 'Thank you for giving me your time. I must let you get back to your guests.' He paused at the door. 'How do they fit in with all this, by the way?' He waved a hand at her work.

'Art therapy. I go over to Gateway two days a week. Slapping clay around gets rid of a lot of tension, and feelings get painted on canvas without the kids realising what's going on. More "amateur psychiatry", as you called it.'

He stood looking down at her, an odd look on

his face.

'I conceded that point. Maybe I wasn't convincing enough. Perhaps what I said needed reinforcing.' He moved slightly, and she didn't know what he was going to do and took a nervous step backwards.

'I was only teasing,' she said hurriedly, and he laughed.

'So was I. What on earth did you imagine I meant?'

She'd thought—and it was a ridiculous thought—that he was going to kiss her. And he knew it. Ros wasn't going to be played with in any cat-and-mouse fashion.

'Go ahead,' she told him coolly. 'I'll lock up . . . and the cloth over the clay needs damping down.'

He went, leaving her to cope with the clay and her own awkwardness before closing up the Stables and going over to put her barely touched supper plate down. There was a cluster of children wheeling round her as soon as she appeared, and it was a moment or two before Ros noticed that Paul was back, talking to Tammy and getting rapidly through a belated supper at the same time. She told the kids she wouldn't be a moment and went over to join them briefly.

'How did they react to the fox?'

'They liked it,' Paul told her. 'And the bloke they wanted to show it to asked to be told of anything else I do. He's from the Design Centre. Can't be bad, can it?'

'Didn't we always say you'd be a big name one

day?' Tammy said happily.

'There's still a gap between liking and buying,' Paul's feet were as always firmly on the ground, no matter how far up in the clouds his imagination might soar.

'I'm glad it went well. I'm about to get the dancing going again now, and you can enjoy the rest of the party—what's left of it.' Ros started back, then called over her shoulder, 'By the way—your friend Dan turned up.'

'My friend who?'

The uneasiness that had seized her in the workshops came flooding back, and Ros retraced her steps.

'Dan. I don't know his other name.'

Paul looked vague. 'I don't even know that one. Everybody I invited was either tied up with something else or away on holiday this week. You must have got it wrong.'

'I'm sure I haven't. He talked about you. I thought he might be a customer or something.' She was scanning faces rapidly. 'He's here somewhere. I've just been——' She bit back the words she had been going to say. Just been talking far too much to someone who seemed to have come out of nowhere and now disappeared off the face of the earth. The leather jacket had gone from the gatepost, and there was no elegant dark head standing out above the laughing, chattering guests. 'He must have gone. He said he had to leave early,' she ended lamely.

'Come *on*, Ros. We want to do some more dancing.' Debra, her face flushed now, was actually pushing for the activity she had been so against.

'Where's your partner?' Ros asked, not very hopefully.

'He had to go. He said Paul would dance with me. Will you, Paul?'

So he had known Paul was back, and yet he hadn't bothered to speak to him. Ros frowned.

'What did he say his name was, Debs?' She was sure she hadn't got it wrong, but the whole business was so silly that she had to check.

'Dan. I don't know Dan what. He's going to send me a book. He told me so.'

Ros shrugged helplessly at Paul. 'Oh, well . . . maybe you'll remember somebody you gave a casual invitation to. I'd better get on.'

It went on bugging her through the next two dances while she automatically called out the routines.

He had know Paul—known about his wood-carvings, too. And he'd known her own name. So, since she didn't know him from Adam, and Paul claimed not to do so either, who on earth was it who had been so interested in their work? And she'd told him all that about Max, too. If poor old Max hadn't died, she'd be terrified now that she'd given all that away to someone who might be some kind of social worker.

A repeat of the last dance was asked for, and no calling was required second time around. Alan wandered over to stand with her at the turntable.

'You look very fetching tonight,' he said. 'I think you should always wear that flower thing in your hair.'

The expression on his face brought back Dan's shrewd observation and an accompanying embarrassment that this was yet another bit of knowledge about her that he had acquired.

'Come off it, Alan!' she said briskly. 'You're the last person to want your staff wandering around like a load of latter-day hippies.'

'Well, maybe not in school, then,' he gave in with a grin. Then he added hurriedly, 'Ros—there's something I want to talk to you about. When can we have a quiet word?'

'Now—if you can do it in what's left of this track before I need to do any more calling.' She deliberately didn't rise to the threatened intimacy in his tone.

He looked round. 'It isn't the sort of thing I want to talk about here. Too many ears flapping. Is there any chance of your coming back to the school with me when we leave? We could have a quiet coffee when the kids are stowed for the night.'

Ros snatched at a legitimate excuse. 'I can't really walk out on all the clearing up, Alan. It's largely through me that we've got the kids here this year, and Paul and Tammy have shared all the expenses as well as the preparations. Maybe it could wait until next Saturday after the fête? I know there isn't much chance on school days.'

'I suppose so. There's no real rush.' He was so good-humoured, his calm, unflappable nature so eminently suited to the job he did. 'It's been a good party,' he went on. 'Those faces out there are the real thanks, but I must add mine. You put well over a hundred per cent into your job.'

'Look who's talking!' The threat of an intimacy she wasn't sure she was ready for postponed, Ros smiled at Alan. He was a thoroughly nice person, and they did have a lot in common. She wasn't sure that that was enough to make her allow their relationship to move on from the largely professional with a smattering of social mixing thrown in to something more personal. There ought to be more of a spark between them for that, not just a comfortable warmth.

She let thoughts of the gatecrasher drift to the back of her mind. If gatecrasher he was . . . It wasn't the sort of party to invite it, and neither had he seemed the sort of person to do it.

It wasn't until the clearing up was over and Ros was having a bedtime mug of chocolate with Tammy and Paul round the almost dead bonfire in the yard that the subject cropped up again.

'Have you remembered who the mysterious tall, dark stranger might have been?' she asked Paul lightly.

He shook his head. 'I didn't ask anybody I just knew vaguely . . . only people like Mike and Geoff and the Robertsons.' His face in the red glow from the embers suddenly grew alert. 'Hang on a minute, though. That cliché of yours about "tall and dark" . . . Was he really big? Nearly a head above me? The sort of face I'd like to sculpt? Good, strong lines?'

'Sounds like him. He'd got a light grey leather jacket.'

'That's the one. I can't tell you much about him,

though, except that he was turning into the drive as I was leaving it, and he stopped and got out to ask if it was a through road. I told him no, it just went to the Dower House and the Stables, unless you were following the right of way on foot, which he obviously wasn't. He remarked about the fox under my arm—I hadn't got a big enough piece of paper to wrap it completely —and we started talking about it. That's all I know about him. He didn't say where he was wanting to go.'

'Did you tell him my name?'

'Of course not. Why should I?'

'What about yours?'

'Nor my own.' Paul frowned a moment. 'But the paper was from a parcel with my name and address on it in big enough letters. I suppose he could have got it from that.'

'Well, he certainly knew both. You know what's just occurred to me? He could be involved with Max's estate in some way.'

'Then why on earth didn't he say so?' Tammy asked.

'Perhaps he didn't think it was exactly an opportune time. It didn't stop him pumping me as hard as he could, though. He probably wanted to get an idea of how awkward we'd be likely to be about getting out of the Stables.' Ros drained her mug, annoyed that this solution to the mystery hadn't occurred to her sooner.

'As if we would!' Tammy's honest face was outraged. 'We've always known it couldn't last for ever. We've had three lovely years . . .' She smiled at Paul. 'Haven't we?'

'And now I'm afraid it looks as though they're over.' Ros kicked a smouldering branch back into the embers of the fire. 'Well—that's the mystery explained, I imagine. No doubt we'll soon be hearing officially from Max's solicitors.' She gazed into the fire for a moment. 'He didn't exactly say anything that was untrue, I suppose. I did all the assuming, and he didn't contradict me.'

'That makes him all the sneakier, doesn't it?' Tammy said.

'Typical legal attitude.' Paul yawned. 'Well, I'm for bed. Goodnight, you two.'

'I'm coming up as well.' Tammy drifted off into the house with him and Ros followed. She was last to leave the kitchen, rinsing the three mugs and standing them on the rack, thinking as she did so that a cup of chocolate wasn't really equal to taking away the faintly unpleasant taste left by what ought to have been a wholly pleasant evening.

She was too tired to sort out whether her sense of disappointment was due to sadness at having to leave the Stables, or to an irrational feeling of letdown that a man who had worked such charming wonders with Debra should have done so only to cover up his ulterior motives.

CHAPTER TWO

IT WAS half-way through the following week when the official-looking letter stamped with the address of Carter and Wainwright, Solicitors, on the reverse of the long white envelope arrived for Ros.

She was alone at the Stables that day. Paul had been called up to the Design Centre for a further inspection of some of his larger pieces. Tammy had taken the opportunity to go up to London with him and call on the buyers at several large stores with samples of her own work.

So there was no one with whom Ros could share the plummeting of her feelings when she read the brief request to telephone Mr Wainwright's secretary and arrange an appointment at her earliest convenience.

Mr *D*. Wainwright. So that was it. Mr D. Wainwright of Saturday's unprofessional conduct. He would certainly hear how she felt about that, Ros thought grimly as she dialled the number on the letter-heading.

The young-sounding secretary who answered was pleasant enough, and it was certainly no fault of hers after all, so Ros veiled her displeasure. Mr Wainwright was anxious to see Miss Howard as soon as possible, the girl said. In fact—if she happened to be free that very day, it would be possible to fit her in at eleven-thirty that morning, if that wasn't rushing things too much.

It wasn't a Gateway day, and Ros, knowing that delaying tactics would only drag out the regrettable change that lay ahead for all of them, agreed.

She got out a black and white patterned silk dress for the occasion—something sombre to suit the sombre proceedings—then washed her hair and sat outside in the courtyard in the sun for it to dry. Daks, the golden retriever they had jointly bought but who was convinced he belonged to Ros alone, sat at her feet, submitting to the distracted pulling of his ears as Ros wondered how many more quiet moments like this were left to her . . . to all of them.

So sure was she of seeing the dark intruder from the Midsummer's Eve party that Ros stopped short with a little involuntary intake of breath when Mr Wainwright's secretary showed her into his office. The man rising from his chair was short, grey-haired, and the wrong age entirely.

'Miss Howard—thank you for coming in to see me at such short notice. David Wainwright. Delighted to meet you,' he said, then, seeing her surprise, 'Is something wrong?'

Ros collected herself. 'No. I was simply expecting you to be someone else. Tell me, Mr Wainwright, did someone from this partnership come to see me incognito last Saturday? There can be no reason for secrecy now, surely? Perhaps it was your partner?'

'Mr Carter? Oh, no . . . I have always dealt with Mr Maxton's affairs myself, and Mr Carter has only played a small part in the business since his stroke last year. My letter was our first initiative in your direction, Miss Howard. Do please sit down. This is a little confusing.'

Ros took the chair he indicated, feeling thrown that the puzzle she had thought explained continued still. Once again it would have to be shelved.

'Well, at least there's no question about why you want to see me,' she said. 'It's about the Stables, isn't it? We've been expecting to hear from you.'

'So Mr Maxton had discussed the terms of his Will with you?'

Ros's blue eyes widened. 'Never. Why should he? We were only friends. There was no stronger link than a great deal of affection between us. I never thought he cared much about what happened after his death, actually. His prime concern was to avoid being sucked into the system and tidied away into some ghastly old people's home. The thought of that appalled him.'

Mr Wainwright looked keenly at her. 'Then it would surprise you to learn that Mr Maxton made a very watertight Will with specific instructions for the disposal of his estate?'

Ros gave a little smile. 'I think I know what you are leading up to. Don't be alarmed. We shall move out of the Stables as soon as you wish. We've been looking around for somewhere else——' and having singularly little success, she thought silently, '—and we won't complicate matters, Mr Wainwright. We've been extremely lucky to have three almost rent-free years in such a place. We've loved every minute of it . . . and we'll always be grateful to Max.'

'And he to you, obviously. Miss Howard—the terms of the Will ensure that you can go on living there, not as tenant, but as sole owner of the Stables.'

Ros stared at him, thunderstruck. 'It can't be true. Surely the Stables must go with the rest of the estate?'

'That would be desirable, yes. But Mr Maxton's wishes were quite clear. The house and any monies to his nephew, Daniel, his brother's son. The Stables to you.'

'He'll contest it of course, this Daniel Maxton.' The mystery existed no longer.

'Ah—you've heard of him, then?'

'I've met him. He was the man who turned up when we were having a party last Saturday—no mention of the name Maxton, of course, but he did admit to Daniel. No doubt he wanted to see what he was up against.'

The solicitor frowned his unspoken disapproval, then said drily, 'Well, there's no question of contesting. The codicil was quite in order—witnessed somewhat oddly by two of the council's refuse collectors, but quite legally.'

Ros struggled with a sudden mixture of laughter and tears.

'Oh, dear old Max! He always did everything the unexpected way—all through his life, I gather. He died in his own way—and now this.'

Max had been in the old summer-house when

they found him, his head turned towards the south facing doorway. Perhaps he'd seen one last, lovely sunrise through it. However his last hours had passed, they had left a look of such quiet contentment on his face that Ros and Paul and Tammy had felt nothing but happiness for him. They couldn't imagine how he had made his way there, though. For months he had been wheeled through the garden in an antiquated invalid chair from the attic, but somehow on that last morning he'd managed the path and the three shallow steps on his own. Always the individual, Ros thought affectionately, and now he'd done this for her.

Mr Wainwright broke into her thoughts.

'Mr Daniel Maxton would like to see you for a quiet talk this afternoon—his own words—if possible. He phoned to make tentative arrangements while you were on your way here, or I would have made this appointment for after lunch to save you two journeys. He asked to meet you here "on neutral ground" as he phrased it. Will that be possible?'

'Oh, yes,' Ros said softly, and the softness of her voice in no way disguised a steely determination. 'I'll see him.'

She cycled back to the Stables in a daze and changed into her old jeans and paint-spattered pink sweatshirt. She would have to change again in little more than an hour, but she had a great urge to walk about her land—*her land*—like a cat marking its territory, and the silk dress would snag so easily.

She put a hunk of cheese in French bread and ate

it as she went through the house, her free hand touching the walls of each room as if to reassure herself that they were solid and real and hers. She wandered round the courtyeard, in and out of the workshops, with Daks following her, his wet nose nudging at her hand in puzzlement at this oddest of walks.

Ros knelt down and ruffled his coat.

'Yes, it's all very strange, Daks, I know, boy. Come on. There's just time for a proper walk through the woods if we're quick.'

The retriever went bounding gracefully ahead of her, the habit of the past months making him slip through the gap in the Dower House fence in spite of Ros's call instead of going as she had intended along the right of way through the woods.

She squeezed through after him, knowing full well where she would find him, and sure enough, as she reached the summer-house he came whining softly to meet her from its interior.

'I know, boy.' She rubbed his head as she spoke. 'He's not here, is he? And you can't understand it.'

The cushions on the battered old cane chaise-longue were still indented where Max had been lying, and it was this that brought all the emotion of the day rushing to the surface.

It was the very last moment she would have chosen to have someone see her, but a footstep crunched on the gravel path and with a quick dash at her eyes Ros was forced to turn round and see Daniel Maxton standing there. In his dark grey suit and crisp white shirt he was immaculate in the face of her scruffiness, composed in contrast with her raw vulnerability. His eyes were as unfathomable as ever, and there was a slight smile playing on his lips.

'So much for attempting to meet on neutral ground, Ros,' he said wryly.

'At least this time we both know exactly to whom we are speaking—and why.' Ros summoned up no answering smile. 'I had no idea you'd taken over the house already or I wouldn't be here. Wouldn't be here anyway, if Daks hadn't slipped through the fence from habit.'

There was a subtle change in him from that first contrived meeting. Then he had been questioning, receptive to what she had to say. Now he was on his own territory in every sense. The man in charge.

'Excuse me,' she said coldly, dragging what shreds of dignity she could around herself as she moved towards him, indicating that he was blocking her exit. 'We have a meeting this afternoon. I won't trespass any longer.'

He didn't move. 'I rather expected you to be on your high horse about Saturday once you knew who I was. But you must admit that you did rather offer me the chance to look round incognito on a plate, didn't you?'

'And you took it and used it to pump me of as much information as you could. Not exactly the behaviour of a gentleman, was it?'

'I wasn't sure then that you merited gentlemanly treatment. But since you patently had nothing to hide except a very warm heart, there was no real harm done.'

'I knew I had nothing to hide, but you didn't. That puts a different complexion on what you did.'

'Exactly.' He lowered one hand for Daks's curious inspection and, when it was approved, played gently with the long, feathery ears, still looking calmly at Ros. 'Does it surprise you, in the light of what you must know since your appointment with Mr Wainwright this morning, that I should want to see what it was about a group of rather unconventional tenants that induced my uncle to divide his estate to the benefit of one of them?'

Anger seethed in Ros. 'Perhaps not,' she said curtly. 'And similarly, if I had been in the position of advantage, I might well have been equally curious to discover as much as I could about a relative who didn't seem to exist until the sharing-out process began.'

The dark eyes sparked for a moment. Only for a moment, and the smooth reply followed without hesitation. 'Ah—but then, you see, my uncle's Will had apparently been made in my favour since shortly after my birth. The clause referring to you, on the other hand, was drawn up when he was old and frail. Anyone would have felt a passing curiosity as to why that should be.' He raised an imperious hand to stem the protest she was about to make. 'Don't worry. Any questions I might have wanted to ask on that score have been adequately answered not only by you, but by Dr Ward. Undoubtedly you gave my uncle security and peace of mind in his last years. I fully accept that he had cause to wish to reward you.'

'Then there seems very little for us to talk about,' Ros said stiffly.

'If that were so, I wouldn't have made time to see you.' He glanced at his watch. 'Under the circumstances it seems ridiculous to go to Wainwright's office. I'll call him to say what's going on.'

'As you wish,' Ros told him coldly. When he turned to go back towards the Dower House, she irritably reached forward and grabbed Daks's collar. The damned dog was fawning around this unforgivable man as though he were a long-lost friend.

Daniel Maxton's voice, whether intentionally or not, mocked her.

'A friendly animal you've got there.'

'He's young—and totally without discrimination.'

He gave her a withering sideways glance. 'When we met last Saturday, I had the impression of talking to a reasonable adult. It would be a pity—now we've got to the point of talking business—to find that I was mistaken on that score.'

He lengthened his stride, and Ros followed in considerable mental discomfort. It wasn't often that she caught herself out in the sort of childish behaviour she had just indulged in, and she had at once begun to reproach herself for it. A certain amount of annoyance was justified under the circumstances, but not on the level of that silly remark about Daks.

Reason made her see that Daniel Maxton had

every right to question the arrangements of the Will.
Suspicion made her debate whether he wasn't
simply engaged in a clever softening of the
opposition before he got round to whatever he
wanted to talk about. Either way, she would gain
nothing by losing her self-control.

In the house he looked impatiently round the
room Max had lived in.

'There must be the means of making tea
somewhere in all this chaos if one knew where to
look for things. So far I haven't seen beyond the
mound of papers that have to be gone through.'

'I know my way around,' she told him. 'I'll go
and get a tray.' It was as good a way as any of letting
herself calm down, and of checking whether she
really looked as bad as she felt she did.

The cloudy mirror in the panelled hall reassured
her a bit. Her hair was its usual, gleaming frame to a
face that never relied too much on make-up and was
now not unpleasantly flushed by her feelings. And if
her clothes were only too obviously working
gear—well, Daniel Maxton knew what she did, so
there was no need to apologise for them.

The calming-down process went a bit awry,
though, as by the time Ros returned with the tea-
things she was feeling not so much calm as slightly
resentful of her own willingness to take on what he
probably considered to be woman's work. She put
the tray down pointedly near him, and went to sit at
a slight distance, leaving him to pour.

This he did without any sign of resentment, and
as he handed her a cup he said pleasantly, 'I

decided while you were out there to embark on
something that may begin by sounding like a
curriculum vitae, but which does have a point, I
assure you. It will leave us understanding each other
a little better, I think.'

Ros stirred her tea, her attention caught despite
herself. 'Go on, then. I'm listening.'

He drank deeply, not hurrying. 'That's good!
I've spent a couple of hours among some rather
dusty papers. Now, you've heard of Commax
Systems?'

'The computer people? Who hasn't?' Suddenly
the link between his name and the last syllable of the
company logo struck Ros. 'Are you saying that
that's you? Your company?'

'One of them. My first venture . . . I happened to
be in the right place at the right time, and it took off.
The obvious parallel companies, D.M. Software and
Maxton Associates—a consultancy service—grew
almost as quickly, and they're both operating on a
national level now. I won't bore you with the rest,
though there are more. And despite that look on
your face which I can read only too well, this is no
ego-trip. I'm only telling you so that you can be
reasonably assured that I have no need of Max's
money, and as far as I'm concerned, being involved
in his estate is something I could well do without.'

Ros was thinking hard. 'So just why did Max
bother to involve you, then?'

'Only Max knew that. The fact that I know so
little about him and his reasons explains my non-
appearance on the scene until now. To be frank, I

knew of my uncle's existence, but that's about all. Originally he and my father were in business together—a cycle company here in the Midlands. My father was never cut out for it, and as Max lived for nothing else they were totally incompatible as partners. I don't know the details . . . only the outcome. My father left, taking nothing from the business, and ended up with a smallholding in Cumberland, completely happy, though far from wealthy. Max found not too much in the way of personal happiness, I imagine, but he made a considerable success of the business, though from what I gather his eccentric approach to investment took care of most of that. Maybe to begin with he felt that he'd cheated my father out of his share. I just don't know. But he arranged his affairs in my favour in the early days, and though he obviously had subsequent thoughts, as the clause relating to you shows, he never actually altered the main part of his Will. So there we are. I'm really no more a villain than you are.'

He smiled at her, a smile of such warmth that Ros was briefly dazzled until she remembered his effect on Debra. Warning lights flashed. He's setting out to charm you, she told herself . . . and he's got a reason for it which you haven't been told yet.

'It really isn't any of my business,' she said cautiously. 'I was caught off balance in the summer-house. You know that was where Max died?' He nodded, and she went on, 'It threw me a little, that's all. I'd be happy if you could forget everything I said.'

He looked steadily at her. 'But we can't forget, can we, that I own this house and you own the Stables?'

Ah . . . and there we have it. You want the lot, in spite of your protestations, Ros thought as he went on to ask, 'Tell me—did you by any chance see and rather wish you had the Stables? Or did it happen exactly as you told me—by pure chance?'

'Exactly as I told you.'

'So if you were offered compensation above and beyond the value of the Stables themselves—more than enough to buy yourself similar property somewhere else—to have it custom-built, for that matter—it would be a pretty fair deal?'

Ros resisted the wave of forceful persuasion she could feel emanating from him with all her might.

'Forgive me if I ask one thing. Why?' she said.

He smiled again, put down his cup and rose, stretching.

'I might have known you'd come right to the crux of the matter. Come outside with me and I'll show you.'

She followed him until he stood aside to let her precede him through the french windows, conscious of the energy in his broad-shouldered, tall frame. It seemed to exude from him in almost tangible waves when he switched on the power, as he had done now. It was a force-field that she would have to resist with all her strength if he were not to sweep her off her feet completely and carry her along in the current of whatever it was he wanted to do.

He strode a little way down the lawn and stopped,

Daks leaping round him, to look back at the house.

'One company interest of mine that I haven't mentioned until now is the renovation of old, neglected properties. The last place I dealt with was similar in period and design to the Dower House here. We built out at the rear—two wings, you can see how that would be possible here—to give extra bedroom and dining-room space, and turned a derelict barn of a place no one wanted or could afford to live in into a very successful country club with bags of olde-worlde charm and atmosphere.'

Ros hid her appalled reaction to the thought of this beautiful old house, a place she had grown to love so much, being gutted and changed in such a way.

'I see. And how far would these proposed wings extend?' She managed to ask the question with apparent interest and not the revulsion she felt.

'About as far as the summer-house. That would have to go, of course,' he said with matter-of-fact callousness. 'No point in turning the place into a shrine, as Max—businessman that he was in his prime—would be the first to emphasise.'

'So how do I come into this?' Ros brought herself to look at him, and those dark, inscrutable eyes held hers.

'The other property we developed had no outbuildings to speak of. As soon as I saw the Stables I knew exactly how they could be used. A central pool area. Changing rooms and a gymnasium and the rest where the workshops and house are. The original shell is sound—attractive . . . it would take everything needed for a superb leisure complex. The National Exhibition Centre being almost on the doorstep, this is the ideal spot for an overspill hotel with the right facilities.'

He was waiting for a reply.

'You've obviously thought it all out, in spite of your alleged lack of interest in the property,' she said pointedly.

'I'm involved in it, like it or not. The house is there. I've got to do something with it.' And something, in his world, meant turning the Dower House into a marketable travesty of its lovely old self, while her beloved Stables . . .

'As far as you're concerned,' he went on persuasively, 'I would have three estimates of the value of the Stables from property valuers of your choice, and give you a mark-up of twenty-five per cent on the highest. Bearing in mind the fact that as access is not stipulated in the Will and without that the Stables would be virtually unsaleable on the open market, I think you would find any legal expert urging you to take up the offer.'

Ros digested the threat veiled in his pleasantly expressed words. Take his offer now, or lose out altogether in the long run. No doubt he could make life very difficult over the question of access, certainly as far as vehicles were concerned. Mr Wainwright didn't appear to have foreseen that. But surely he couldn't do anything about the right of way that went straight past the courtyard entrance? As long as that existed, and she could get in and out on foot, he wasn't as all-powerful as he thought.

'I'm sure you're right,' she said slowly. 'About the advice, I mean.' Ros was deep in thought, but not along the lines this cold-blooded tycoon was no doubt convinced he had laid down.

'Think about it,' he said magnanimously. 'Speak to Wainwright. See what transpires as far as estimates are concerned. I don't want to rush you into any decision.'

He thought he'd got her. She could see confidence oozing from every pore as they returned to the house.

'Oh . . . I don't really have to think,' Ros said gently. 'Perhaps if I give you a little of my own curriculum vitae, you'll see that in a position like this there's only one answer for me.'

She felt malicious satisfaction in the way she'd worded that. It could be taken both ways—acceptance or refusal of his offer, and she could see from the way he settled in a chair again, polite interest on his face, the quick glance at his watch almost too fast for her to observe it, that he took it for granted she meant the former.

'I've never really settled anywhere,' she began. 'I was only two when my father made us pull up our roots for the first time. And so it went on. There was always a good reason. My father was an ambitious man. His job meant being willing to move around if he wanted to get on, and every move brought financial rewards. Bigger and better houses for shorter and shorter times. Nobody had any choice in the matter. If I wept for the friends I left behind, that was life. Material rewards should make up for it.

And if I learned in time that it was safer not to make friends, then that was a good lesson to learn, my father thought. People one didn't love could be left behind quite easily. If your way of life had to consider someone else's desires and happiness, it held you back.'

There was a little frown on Daniel Maxton's forehead now, as though he were not so sure what she was telling him.

She deliberately gave him false hope. 'And now you are offering me the chance to buy my own house—even to have one built to my own specification.' She paused, savouring the pause, 'I ought to seize it. I'm sure you're right when you tell me that will be the advice I shall be given.' Her voice shook slightly as she at last gave her feelings rein. 'But Max got there first, you see. He had three years before you came along with your plans and your unrefusable offers and your cold, calculated schemes. Max let me grow into a home of my own during those three years, with people I couldn't stop myself loving and a place that against all the lessons of my upbringing grew to mean roots and belonging and everything I thought I'd never let myself feel about any place. And now he's made it mine for good.'

She stood, confronting him passionately as she poured out her feelings, and Daniel Maxton rose with her, his eyes on hers.

'I want no part in your schemes for this place. I don't want the heart torn out of those three years. I want that heart to go on beating in my life. I can't stop you doing what you want with the poor old Dower House. But I can and I will stick right in your path as far as the Stables are concerned. You can forget about buying me off. And you can forget about your lousy leisure centre. The Stables are mine, and they stay as they are.'

To her complete chagrin, he burst out laughing.

'You impossible woman! What brand of po-faced obstinacy makes an otherwise rational human being turn down the chance of a lifetime like this? You can't be serious?'

Ros's fair skin flushed with fury. 'Never more so. You must find it difficult to understand, looking down from your cut-throat world of high finance, that money can't buy everything. But it certainly can't buy me.'

His laughter faded. 'And you're under no misapprehension about the true value of this property of yours? You know that if I don't buy it, no one else will? You can't argue away the question of access with high-mindedness.'

His taunting smile had none of the charm he had tried on her earlier.

'You couldn't buy me . . . and you won't scare me,' Ros said sturdily. 'And now, since there's nothing more to be said, I'll be off.'

'Oh, but there is!' He was at the door before her, his arm barring the way. Ros felt again that strange sense of power in him, and in spite of her determination she felt a tingle of fear run up her spine. His eyes narrowed as he looked down on her. 'Are you someone who means what she says?' he asked strangely.

Her blue eyes blazed defiantly. 'I certainly am.'

'Then I'll quote your own immortal words at you. "Anyone who writes off a thing without giving it a go is a bit of a wally. If you do it and then decide it's not for you, fair enough. But you should at least give it a chance." Well? Eyewash to get a kid to do something she didn't want to do? Sheer hypocrisy on your part? Or do you believe it?'

Caught in a trap of her own making, Ros floundered. 'I believe it—but surely you're not saying it's applicable in this case? That I should sell first to see what it's like, then change my mind and hope you'll let me buy back? Do you really think I'm so naïve?'

'I'm saying you should weigh up all the pros and cons. Hear all the arguments for and against. Give me time to open your narrow field of vision up a bit. Or maybe give yourself the chance to convince me that you're right. Anything wrong with that?'

'Delaying tactics!' Ros snapped.

'Sensible exploration of the situation,' he countered, quick as a flash. 'The course you urged on a child in your care, remember, and which you've just said you believe in.'

She hesitated, and in that moment knew that he had won—if not the battle, at least this first skirmish—on sheer tactics.

'So you'll talk about it . . . think about it . . . follow your own advice?' He was quick to seize the advantage.

'I shall end up at the same decision.'

'Maybe, but at least you won't have made it out of blind prejudice.'

'I can think of nothing you can say or do to make me change my mind.'

'I can show you Tindall's to begin with: the place you claim, without having set eyes on it, that you couldn't bear the Dower House to end up resembling. And you can also get some impartial professional opinions on the situation.'

It had caught her, that force-field she had recognised but been so powerless to resist. But she would go on fighting it.

'You'll find you've wasted your time,' she said, reaching for Daks's collar.

'It's a risk I'm willing to take.'

Ros gave the dog a sharp pull and made for the hall.

'I'll be in touch—very soon,' he called after her, then she heard him hurrying in pursuit. 'By the way . . . this is a book I promised Debra. Perhaps you'll pass it on.'

Ros took the parcel and left. She would have liked to be able to condemn him for a broken promise, but he had proved her wrong.

'Where were you when I needed support?' she said crossly to Daks's questioning face. 'Spellbound or something?'

She let go of his collar and watched him happily snuffling his way back along the path. Then, as she thought how the tables had been so neatly turned on her, honesty compelled her to add, 'You and me both, Daks, it seems.'

CHAPTER THREE

IT RAINED in the late afternoon, and, as Ros rushed around placing buckets and pans under the leaky parts of the roof that they had never felt justified in informing Max about, she told herself what a fool she was. Who but a fool would do anything but jump at the chance of brand-new, problem-free living premises handed out like a gift from the gods? And here she was, turning the lot down in favour of a place that needed a fortune spent on it—a fortune she hadn't got.

At that moment, with the leaden skies pressing down against a background chorus of water plunking on metal and the steady drip from the trees that in this light seemed oppressive, not friendly, she had no problem convincing herself that she was mad.

But the sun came out, and from the bedroom window the trees with their wet leaves were a dazzle of shining light. The old slates on the stable roofs glowed in an artist's palette of subtle colours like pebbles in a stream—and somehow they'd get the roof fixed . . . of course they would!

The sight of the Bentley Continental Convertible shooting down the drive away from the Dower House with Dan Maxton at the wheel completed the

firming of her resolution to hang on to the Stables.
She recognised the car because it was the model her
father had been driving the last time she saw him
when he flashed out of her life, and out of her
mother's, for good. Everything she had sensed about
Dan Maxton's philosophy of living seemed
symbolised by the car. A fortune to buy, a fortune to
run—a sheer self-indulgence. The badge of the
successful man who wanted to flaunt his
success—the sort of man who was anathema to her.

She heard Tammy and Paul come back in the
small hours in the noisy little van they all shared,
and was tempted to get up and tell them at once, but
the quiet way they were talking and the soft chuckles
that punctuated their conversation made her hold
back for some reason. And it was rather nice to
snuggle under her duvet with her secret, thinking of
the surprise they would get in the morning.

When Ros did tell them, she was glad she had
waited, because their reaction was not at all what she
had expected. Certainly it would have kept her
awake rather than sent her satisfied to sleep.

Of course they were surprised and delighted at
first to hear of Max's legacy. It was when she got
round to the purchase offer from Dan Maxton and
her rejection of it that it began to be obvious that
they were not in agreement with her.

'You ought to take it, Ros,' Paul said reflectively.
'That question of access really is a big one.'

'Even with the right of way?'

'He could put someone in the lodge to make

damned sure it was as difficult as possible for us. No deliveries. No kids from Gateway in their special minibus. No van of ours going in and out, for that matter.'

'I'm not going to let him bulldoze me out of this place. It's ours,' Ros said mutinously.

'It's *yours*,' Tammy corrected.

Ros stared at her. 'Is that it? Are you angry it was left to me rather than to all of us? I consider it ours—you know that.'

'Not angry at all. Glad, really,' Tammy said levelly. 'At least it's your decision now, and it's obvious we'd disagree about it if it involved the three of us. You did masses more for Max than anyone else, anyway, so don't be stupid. And another thing——' she added, 'I wouldn't want the worry of the upkeep of this place, much as I love it. We've been able to pretend so far that anything crumbling under our noses wasn't our responsibility, but that can't go on now, can it?'

Ros felt flattened by their attitude. 'I thought we'd be celebrating, not arguing,' she said dully.

Paul reached across the table and chucked her under the chin.

'Of course we're glad. But we want you to do the right thing. Max wanted to give you something, but at his age and in his state of health, he wasn't up to seeing that there were no snags. Now someone offers to make sure you *do* benefit permanently. Look at it rationally, Ros.'

'There's always a rational reason for going after money, isn't there?' Ros said bitterly.

'That's your complexes talking!' Tammy said, not unkindly.

'And I'm stuck with them.'

'There's something else . . .' Paul said slowly. 'You speak as though we'll always be here, but if you think about it, it's not going to be like that, is it? Sooner or later someone's going to move out. Maybe it'll be us before you. In that case, it wouldn't be fair of us to urge you to keep this place on just because it suits us now, would it?'

Shades of the old panic she thought she'd got under control flickered in Ros. 'You're not thinking of moving, are you?'

'Not right now,' Tammy said. 'But you've got to see Paul's right. It could happen. Do at least try to think it out sensibly, Ros.'

Paradoxically, with everyone professing to care about her interests, Ros had never felt so much on her own. They had always sorted out problems as a trio. Now it was Paul and Tammy—if not exactly against her, at least apart from her.

She stood up, tossing her hair back impatiently. 'Well, we can't go on talking about it all day. They'll be looking out for us at Gateway. You haven't forgotten about the fête?'

'Would we—with workshops full of bits and pieces we've been making for weeks?' Tammy said, jumping up. 'I'm going to start loading my stuff.'

When she had gone out, Paul said, 'I shan't be able to stay at the school all day, I'm afraid, Ros. I've got to go in to the Ikon to tell them about yesterday.'

'Oh, Paul! How utterly selfish of me!' Ros said shamefacedly, jarred into remembering by the mention of the gallery's name. 'I didn't even ask. How did you get on?'

He grinned modestly. 'Not too bad. And you did have a fair bit to occupy your mind. They're putting two of my pieces on show in London at the Centre, and I'm going to be mentioned in various bits of literature, including the Country Workshops booklet.'

'That's marvellous!' Ros exclaimed. 'Just think—we'll probably have visitors from the States rolling up to look round and buy your work!'

'If they can get here—that's the question, isn't it?' he reminded her quietly. 'It might be safer to have the Ikon's address inserted until we know what's going to happen.'

Ros sighed. He was only stating the obvious. 'What about Tammy?'

'Nothing definite, but Liberty's buyer is going to write to her. They seemed genuinely interested, she thought. All in all, a pretty good day for each of us.'

But not without its complications, Ros thought. She went up to her room and slipped on the blue linen dress she was wearing for the fête. White beads and ear-rings made her look far more festive than she felt, and with an impatient 'What the hell?' she grinned at herself in the mirror and determined to brood no more.

The school hall was already buzzing when they arrived, and it wasn't difficult to forget everything but the work in hand.

'Someone sent this for you,' she told Debra, who was helping on the Arts and Crafts stall, taking Dan Maxton's parcel out of the box containing her pictures.

The child's face lit up. 'I knew Dan wouldn't forget!' She tore off the wrapping quickly and Ros saw that there was a note in with the book, which Debra read avidly before proudly showing off the hardback copy of *The Lion, the Witch and the Wardrobe.*

The fête was well supported and business was brisk. By the time Paul left at two-thirty, most of the things on their stall had been sold.

'Do you think I could slip off too?' Tammy asked. 'I could do with a lift into town as long as Paul's going that way. Do you mind, Ros? What about getting home?'

'I expect Alan will run me back. I've got to see him when it's over—and in any case there's not going to be anything to take home, with a bit of luck,' Ros said. Alan had already reminded her twice of his wish to talk, and she was dreading yet another problem to add to the ones that had already appeared on the scene.

'You keep sighing. Are you tired?' Debra asked as they waited rather limply behind the almost empty stall.

Ros smiled at the child. 'Just a bit bogged down by a couple of problems. They'll sort themselves out, I expect.'

Debra's thin little face was sympathetic. 'You can borrow my book when I've read it, if you like.'

Ros felt a warm glow at the realisation that Debra

was actually thinking of someone else—a major step in her recovery. 'That's really nice of you. I'd love to read it again. It's one of my favourites.'

'Dan said it was his, too. I can't wait for bedtime. I read a bit when I was having my lunch.'

So the tycoon was a C.S. Lewis fan. On a day of complications, that seemed like another one. Ros would have preferred to share nothing—not even love of a children's book—with the man.

With the hall empty and the children in the dining-room, exhausted over their evening meal, Ros could put off speaking to Alan no longer. She opened the study door with some trepidation as he called, 'Come in!'

'A good day, I think!' she said brightly as she went in. 'We should have boosted the funds quite a bit.'

Alan's face didn't reflect her cheerfulness. 'But almost certainly not by enough,' he said soberly. 'Sit down, Ros. That's what I wanted to talk to you about.' He leaned back dejectedly in his chair. 'In a nutshell, I've been given advance warning that Gateway might be closed down in the not too distant future.'

'Oh, no!' Ros's own feelings were instantly forgotten. 'They couldn't! What would happen to the kids?'

'They'd have to go to Demster's.' Demster's was a big new school for special education south of the city. Ros had been to the opening, and she had found its size daunting after the homely warmth of Gateway. 'It's the old story,' Alan went on.

'Cutbacks all round. We're too small to be cost-effective. Demster's has the room. It's not certain yet, but the fact that the subject has been aired at all to me makes me think it will happen.'

'I'm sorry, Alan. You've worked so hard for this place.' Ros looked at him with genuine sympathy. 'Why do they do these things? Start schemes they can't go on supporting? No one could give our kids a better adjustment to life than you do at Gateway.'

He smiled for the first time. 'You're a good morale-booster, Ros. Actually, I've been more or less told that there will be a place for me at Demster's if it comes to it. Head of one of the "residences", as they call them.' He paused. 'But they'd like it better if I had a wife.'

Ros had been shocked into forgetting her original suspicions about his reason for talking to her. Now she couldn't stop the blush that spread quickly up her cheeks, and Alan didn't pretend not to see it.

'I'm not going to fudge around and make out that I didn't direct that personally at you,' he said, getting up and going over to the window. 'No doubt you think—and quite rightly—that it's a bit abrupt. But it's not really. You must have known that I've had my eye on you for some time, in my own not very dashing fashion.' He turned round, his nice face a mixture of hopefulness, awkwardness and self-deprecation.

Ros's blue eyes looked candidly at him. 'But we don't really know each other, do we? Not in that way.'

'That doesn't prevent me from wanting us to. I'd like to think you felt the same.'

She was determined to be honest. 'I like you,

Alan—a lot. You know that. And I admire you, both for what you do and for what you are. But there would have to be more than that, wouldn't there?'

He smiled as he walked over and stood looking down at her.

'I suppose there are worse starting points than that. At least you're not giving me an adamant "no".'

She pleated a fold of her dress, her golden head bowed. 'I don't quite know what I'm saying—except that you've given me two big subjects to think about. And I must do that.'

'That's all I ask for now. If you could just tell me, when you've thought a bit, whether you'd like to see more of me . . . then we'll take it from there. We've got a lot in common, Ros.'

She smiled at him as she stood. 'I know we have.'

'Some men would have gone about it in a more romantic way. I felt I had to be honest. I didn't want to start on something you couldn't go along with. I'm too fond of you for that. And just to prove that I'm far from being as cold-blooded about it as you may think——'

He took her face in his hands, gently, and bent to kiss her on the lips. Ros closed her eyes and stood quite still, asking herself what she felt. Neither his touch nor the fresh clean smell of his skin was unpleasant. She decided, as Alan let her go and she smiled composedly—too composedly—at him, that it was affection. She didn't in the least mind being kissed by him. But, on the other hand, nor did it do anything world-shattering to compel her to make up her mind about what he had said.

'You'll keep all this to yourself, won't you?' he said.

'I will. You don't need to ask. Goodbye, Alan. And thank you.'

'Thank you?'

'For paying me a big compliment.'

He scanned her face seriously. 'I hope you'll want to return it. Goodbye, Ros.'

She hadn't asked for a lift home because she felt the need for the walk, and for solitude. Her mind felt over-burdened with issues that were all of prime importance, all somehow linked with each other. How simple life had been before Max died—and how unbelievably complex it was now. In a way, everything would be easier if she could elect to spend the rest of her life with Alan. That would dictate the answer to the other issue, because she would live where Alan lived and the Stables would stop being a subject of contention. Perhaps affection and common interests and respect were the good basis for marriage that Alan said they were, but . . .

But. There was always a 'but'. She wanted all that existed between herself and Alan, but she wanted something more. The magic ingredient to lift a relationship out of the comfortably ordinary into the special, the champagne class. Perhaps she wanted too much.

What she most certainly did not want was to find Dan Maxton kicking his heels in the courtyard of the Stables, looking like trouble, albeit elegantly packaged in an Italian-looking suit.

'Where the hell have you been all day? This is the third time I've called,' he said aggressively.

There was quite a lot of tension screaming for an outlet in Ros.

'Is it *really*?' she said with scathing emphasis. 'Well, Mr Maxton, it may interest you to know that there was life before you. My life goes on, in spite of your eruption into it. And it will go on all the more sweetly once you've taken yourself off—which you could start doing right now.'

'Good!' he said surprisingly. 'I like a woman with a bit of spirit. But we have things to do. If your puritan instincts allow you to indulge in something a bit more festive than that rather faded blue thing you're wearing, go and put it on. We're going out.'

Ros stiffened. 'You may be. But I'm not. I've been working hard all day, and all I want now is a bath, a good meal, and a rest.'

'You can have the bath. The meal's laid on—better than anything you could rustle up. And you can sit down to eat it—totally restful. What more could you ask?'

'To be left alone.'

He looked unblinkingly into her hostile face, quite unabashed.

'Rubbish!' How old are you, for crying out loud? Work all day Saturday, then slump in front of the television like an old-age pensioner all evening? It isn't rest you need, it's stirring up.'

'How do you know what I need?' Ros asked in exasperation.

He reached out and spanned her neck, his thumb

and fingers teasingly rocking her face. 'Because every man knows what a pretty thing like you needs!' he said with mock lasciviousness, his velvety brown eyes caressing hers. Then he let her go and added in a matter-of-fact tone, 'And besides, you gave your word to remain open to persuasion. If I can't appeal to your baser instincts, your saintly side will make sure you don't go back on a promise. I've booked a table at Tindall's. You'll find the place very relaxing, as well as surprisingly impressive, I promise.'

'You don't waste time, do you?' Ros said, involuntarily putting her hand up to her neck, which was still strangely tingling from his touch, soft though it had been.

'Time's money.'

'I thought it wouldn't be long before we got back to that theme,' she said tartly.

'You *are* tired!' he said with offensive mock sympathy. 'Go on. Have that bath. Pretty yourself up. I'll go over to the house and be back in an hour. Long enough?'

Ros stared at him. 'You're pretty sure of yourself, aren't you?'

'I've had to be. It becomes a way of life. How about a little smile to help me look forward to the evening? No?'

'That's something you can't order,' Ros said, going towards the door.

'Never mind. It'll be all the more enjoyable for its rarity value once you forget and let one out. *Ciao!*'

The scrape of her key in the lock covered Ros's

unprintable retort.

Whatever else, Dan Maxton certainly had the ability to focus the mind wonderfully. She felt driven by one overwhelming purpose now: to prove him wrong. Wrong about her puritan instincts, as he called them. Wrong about her inability to dress up for an occasion, and above all, wrong about what he obviously considered his God-given power to carry all before him. She would go and see his wretched conversion job on Tindall's . . . but he damn well wasn't going to do one on her.

There was one knock-out of a dress in her wardrobe, made by Tammy, a near-as-dammit copy of a Dior model, but stamped with Tammy's unique touch. It was white silk, fitting like a glove to the hips and flaring out to a mid-calf hem, and with long, clinging sleeves. There were two panels of fine gold embroidery done with Tammy's magic touch, one just below the boat neckline, one at the waist. Ros had made herself ceramic ear-rings to wear with it, a stunning shower of white and gold petals, and she looked, she knew and had been told, out of this world in the outfit. It had the effect of emphasising the gold nimbus of her hair, of making her glow.

Ros narrowed her eyes as she gave a last look at herself, and sprayed a fine mist of Nina on her pulse spots.

'So sucks to you, Mr Maxton!' she said in a way that ill became her reflection. 'And it didn't cost a fortune. Just the materials, and quite a lot of love and effort on Tammy's part.'

The Bentley purred into the courtyard exactly at

the time he had said it would, and when Ros walked
out on her dainty white high heels she was gratified
by Dan's reaction. He had been leaning casually
against the car, but he straightened up, his eyes
widening as he stared at her, a smile spreading
slowly across his face.

'Well . . .' he drawled, 'I suppose I asked for that.
And I'm certainly glad I got it!'

'If there's a compliment hidden away in there
somewhere, thanks!' Ros said as she drifted past
him on her scented cloud to take the passenger seat.

He waited a moment before starting up the
engine, and she could sense him looking at her with
those dark, disturbing eyes.

'There's more to you than meets the eye, isn't
there?' he said at last.

She glanced at him. 'I hope so. I never did go
much for outward appearances.'

He grinned. 'Lady, for someone who doesn't go
much for outward appearances, you've certainly
acted out of character tonight!'

'But you don't really know my character, do
you?' Ros's blue eyes sparkled and she was
strangely exhilarated by the exchange, and by the
feeling that for once she had the upper hand.

'All right. Let's agree that we've a lot to look
forward to . . . and let's go!' He engaged gear
smoothly, and drove out of the yard.

Tindall's was between Stratford and Stow-on-the-
Wold, on the northern fringes of the Cotswolds, and
the Bentley made an effortless affair of the distance.

Stone gate-pillars supported wrought-iron gates

standing open on to a tree-lined drive with smooth emerald lawns. The only sign that they were not halting before the heavy oak door of a private house was the uniformed attendant who came out to drive the Bentley away, presumably to a discreetly hidden car park.

Inside, in spite of the season, a log fire flickered in the huge fireplace, and up in the minstrel's gallery over the end of the hall a girl in a long black dress was playing a selection of light classical music on a piano. Doors stood open, giving glimpses of sitting-rooms where summer flower arrangements were reflected in the highly-waxed surfaces of antique furniture.

The pleasant, mature receptionist came out from behind the knee-hole desk where she had been sitting.

'Mr Maxton—good evening! Good evening, madam. Would you like drinks in the small sitting-room? Or would you like to go straight to your table? Your reservation is in the Mary Arden room, as you asked.'

'Good evening, Mrs Morton,' Dan said. 'I think, since we are slightly earlier than I suggested, we may as well stroll around the house before we eat. Miss Howard is eager to see all we've done here.' He looked calmly at Ros. 'She knows quite a bit about the property under consideration for similar conversion, so she's naturally interested to see what can be done.'

'Of course.' Mrs Morton smiled at Ros. 'If you're faimiliar with the "before" stage, I'm sure you'll be impressed by what Mr Maxton has achieved here, Miss Howard. In the meantime I'll make sure you are expected shortly in the dining-room, sir.'

As they walked up the broad, red-carpeted stairs, the pianist raised a hand and smiled at Dan, looking with veiled curiosity at Ros.

'You'll meet Karen later, I expect,' he said casually, acknowledging the wave but not pausing. 'Now—I want to show you the south bedroom wing, and from there you can look out at the exterior of the north wing to see how well it blends with the rest of the house. We used reclaimed bricks of the period, of course.'

His enthusiasm was evident as he took Ros through a series of faultless bedroom suites, each with its own subtle colour scheme, culminating in the huge four-poster-equipped bridal suite with its white lace draperies and palest pink carpet.

Ros refused to be prodded into expressing opinions as they went around. 'I'm here to look—and that's what I'll do,' she told Dan firmly. 'Afterwards I'll tell you what I think.'

It became obvious to her very soon, though, that as far as the actual conversion of the house was concerned little fault could be found. The new wings, she could see when they stepped out on to the balcony of the bridal suite, did, as Dan had said, fit in with the house. The garden space between them had been planted out as an Elizabethan rose garden with brick paths and box-edged beds of roses whose scent hung heavily on the air. A colonnaded walk ran along the ground floor of each wing, and off it the dining-rooms opened.

The people sitting chatting over before-meal drinks or after-meal coffee in the chintz chairs in the sitting-rooms could have been guests at a private house-party, and as the waiter handed the menu to Ros in the almond green, gilt and white spaciousness of the dining-room, she philosophically decided that she was going to enjoy the meal and worry about opinions and decisions afterwards.

Dan was out to charm again. She was conscious of it at first but, as the meal progressed and the champagne did its insidious work, Ros forgot to maintain her defences, and when he suggested that they joined the dancers on the polished floor which ran the length of the dining-room and extended out into the lantern-lit colonnades, she rose and followed him in a state of dreamy euphoria, slipping into his arms as though she had been doing so all her life.

For a second she wondered incredulously if he could have somehow arranged for their steps to fit together so magically, then she gave herself up to the sheer physical pleasure of it.

Dan was conscious of it, too. When there was a brief pause in the music, he said, his voice deep and seductive in her ear, 'It seems quite wrong that two people who are so physically attuned as we seem to be should disagree about anything, don't you think?'

Ros told herself when she thought about it afterwards, that it was the champagne that answered for her. 'Don't talk about it,' she murmured. 'If you don't, it doesn't exist.'

He smiled and pulled her golden head in to his shoulder as the music started up again. 'Then I won't, little dreamer,' he said, his arms tightening round her.

Karen brought the temperature down effectively. She was standing at their table when they came back to it, her sleek dark head on one side, pouting prettily at Dan in a way that spoke of more than employer/employee relationship.

'When am I going to be invited to see this latest place of yours, then?' she asked, giving Ros only the briefest of acknowledgements as she was introduced.

'Give me a chance!' he said good-humouredly. 'I haven't moved in myself yet. The place has just been gone through today by a gang of cleaners to make it tolerably habitable while I work on the plans on the spot. I'll show you round as soon as may be, Karen.'

Yet. He hadn't moved in yet . . . but he was transferring to the Dower House from whatever penthouse he was currently inhabiting—probably as much to exert pressure on her as to be on the spot for his planning. The thought was wonderfully sobering to Ros as she stood there on the fringes of the conversation.

She pleaded tiredness when Karen had gone, and in the car on the way home Dan put the inevitable question to her.

Ros stared ahead along the twin beams of the headlamps.

'I'm sure you know that dispassionately I can find no fault with the place. It's beautiful. There's no flaw, no tastelessness in what you've done to the original house. But——' she glanced at his serious profile, 'I'm not a dispassionate person. I'm a prejudiced individual. What you've shown me tonight was a paradise for the privileged—the wealthy few who can afford it. If you want to get me out of the Stables, it won't be to make way for that kind of élite playground, attractive though it is.' An idea occurred to her. 'In fact——' she said, turning impulsively in her seat, 'if we're in the business of changing minds, come with me to a place for the unprivileged, and I'll show you something that might change your own thinking. What's sauce for the goose should be sauce for the gander, don't you think?'

They were turning into the Dower House drive, and as he drew the Bentley to a halt outside the courtyard, Dan shot an ironic glance at her.

'Obstinate little devil, aren't you? All right, then. I'm not scared to face my own treatment. What do you want to show me?'

'Something that I'd see some point in moving heaven and earth—and myself—for. Are you free tomorrow, say around eleven?'

'My time is yours. And now I'll see you to the door. I didn't want to drive in and disturb the others at this hour.'

He took her arm as they walked through the shadows of the yard towards the dark windows of the house. As Ros got out her key, wondering if he had coffee in mind and deciding that he wasn't getting any, she felt him turn towards her.

'This has no ulterior motive,' he said, and took

her in his arms so suddenly that she had no time to stiffen into resistance.

The bewildering sensuousness of his kiss, the assured yet gentle exploration of her lips, stirred into instant life a slow, sweet trembling that spread like a potent drug through her veins.

She was so unprepared for the heady surge of unknown feelings that raced through her that if he had not let her go she couldn't bear to think what might have happened.

She could see that he was looking at her, the moonlight revealing the mixture of amusement and teasing question on his face, and she fought to control the breathless weakness in herself.

'I wish you hadn't done that. Heavy-handed sexist persuasion won't get you anywhere,' she said coldly.

'You're too serious by far,' he mocked. 'Didn't I make it clear that that was pleasure, not business? Relax, my little puritan.'

'I'd prefer you to stick to business in future, then.' She struggled to turn the key in a lock that seemed to have disappeared, his lazy chuckle stoking her anger.

'It was a kiss, sweetie. The whole world's doing it.' His hand closed over hers and stilled her trembling fingers to guide the key into place. 'I had no idea it would mean so much to you. Do forgive me!' The mocking note was stronger. 'I shall see you tomorrow.'

Ros leaned against the closed door with Daks whining around her, puzzled by her stillness. The

Bentley purred into life and its sound died slowly away into the darkness. The man at its wheel, no doubt still with traces of his amusement lingering on his dark, self-confident features, didn't know why his kiss had so disturbed her. He didn't know that it was the second kiss of her day . . . and that if the good, honest man who had given her the first had kissed her like that her future would be clear.

Now all she could think was—poor Alan.

CHAPTER FOUR

A VOICE from Tammy's room made Ros jump as she reached the top of the stairs.

'Where have *you* been, with no note of explanation and coming in at this hour? Out with Alan?'

'No.' Ros went into the room and sat on the bed, wanting, but at the same time reluctant, to talk. 'Maxton took me to see a place like the Dower House that he's waved his magic wand over.'

Tammy switched on the lamp and sat up, hugging her knees, eyebrows rising as she saw what Ros was wearing. 'Well—I hope the place lived up to you! You certainly brought out the big guns, didn't you?'

'He implied I might turn up in jeans or something. Anyway, it's a pretty up-market place. I wasn't overdressed.'

'So what did you think of it?'

'Tasteful. Exclusive. Wouldn't exactly cheer if the Dower House ended up like that—but what say do I have in it? It didn't make me want to hand the Stables over, and that was what he was after. Oh . . .' She groaned and flopped back on the bed, staring up at the ceiling. 'Wasn't life simple before this man came along?'

Tammy rested her chin on her knees, staring at Ros, smiling knowingly. 'He really gets to you, doesn't he?'

'I can't bear him . . . can't bear what he stands for,' she amended. 'He thinks he can buy everything . . . places . . . people . . . Into his bottomless pocket, out with the pennies, and everybody's bowing and scraping and tugging their forelocks. Everybody except me.'

'I think you secretly rather like him. You did until you knew who he was, anyway.'

'What if I did? Knowing what someone's really like makes a difference, doesn't it?'

Tammy was smiling irritatingly. 'And you've got to know him that little bit better tonight?'

Ros sat up abruptly. Tammy had no idea just how much she had learned about herself—not just Dan—in the space of one short evening.

'I'm dead beat now, Tam. Let's save the rest until morning. I'm taking him to see Gateway then. Heaven knows why. It seemed like a good idea at the time, but I don't suppose it will say any more to him than his show-place said to me.' She yawned. 'Oh, well . . . 'Night, Tammy.'

She had got as far as the door when Tammy's mischievous voice hailed her. 'Ros——'

'Yes?'

'Your lipstick's smudged. Who's wearing the bit you've lost? Our acquisitive Mr Maxton?'

She collapsed back on the pillows, laughing, as Ros seized a cushion from the cane chair near the door and flung it at her. Ros went over to the mirror, took a tissue and rubbed at her lips. 'That's what I mean. He thinks everything's his for the taking. I soon disillusioned him.'

'How you must have suffered!' Tammy said dramatically, hand to brow. 'Wined and dined and actually kissed by one of the best-looking blokes we've ever had at one of our parties. The heart bleeds! Bet you'd rather have gone to the pictures and had a McDonalds with Paul and me, wouldn't you?'

'*Goodnight!*' Ros closed the door on her irritating friend and went to her own room.

When she had changed into her pink track-suit-type pyjamas, she curled up on the foot of the bed, leaning on the sill of the open window. It was a glorious night now, the moon fully out from behind the clouds, the trees mysterious and silver. She wondered if Dan Maxton had stayed at the Dower House tonight. It hadn't been obvious from the sound of the car which way he had gone.

An owl hooted its ghostly warning. One thing was certain. The only thought he would have of her, if he thought of her at all, would be an amused, maybe gloating recollection of how he had shaken her with a simple goodnight kiss. She would have to do better than that if she were to hold her own against Dan Maxton.

In the cool early morning Ros bathed and put on her decent pair of jeans and a yellow sweatshirt, pulling her hair back mercilessly and anchoring it with a rubber band. The 'let's score by jazzing ourselves up' line had got her nowhere, only into trouble. Today would be a no-nonsense, straightforward attempt to see if there was any heart at all inside that goldmine of a man.

She went out to the workshop and threw half a dozen bowls for the Woodland series, then, when she had removed her smock and cleaned herself up, she made a list of things she had to do. See Mr Wainwright. Get estimates of the value of the Stables. She looked in Yellow Pages and rang three estate agents to make appointments. The sooner that was done, the sooner she could say that she'd acted, considered, and come back to the same decision: to stay put at the Stables.

The first thing Dan did when he turned up, casually dressed in an oatmeal cashmere sweater and light brown trousers, was frown at her severe hairstyle.

'I don't think this is really necessary,' he said, deftly snapping the rubber band so that her hair tumbled down on to her shoulders. 'Bad for the hair, tight rubber,' he said firmly.

I am not going to be ruffled, Ros told herself.

'Really? Good of you to be concerned.' He was wearing sunglasses and she reached up to remove them. 'Allow me to reciprocate. It isn't really bright enough to warrant these—and surely you're not an image-seeker?' The hinge of the glasses caught in his hair and she had to fumble to free them.

'That's better. I can see that blush of yours in all its glory now,' he said while she struggled.

'Coffee before you go?' Tammy called from the kitchen doorway, her face bright with unashamed curiosity.

'I'm in your partner's hands—quite literally,' Dan said composedly.

'Oh, shut up!' Ros exploded. Then, to Tammy, 'No, we ought to get off, thanks. I've a lot to do today and I'm sure Mr Maxton's empire will be calling. I mustn't trespass too much on his time.'

Tammy withdrew prudently.

At the top of the drive, as they paused before turning into the main road, Dan said, 'So where are we going?'

'About two miles west round the bypass. We're going to my school—Gateway. I'll tell you when we're nearly there.'

'I see.' He didn't ask further questions, and in no time at all they were parking near the main entrance.

Alan, who was chugging to and fro on the sit-on lawnmower, waved a greeting. Ros waved back. 'Unlike Tindall's with its hordes of staff, the headmaster here has to muck in and keep the grounds tidy, you'll note,' she said.

Dan didn't reply until they were through the doors, then he stopped. 'One moment. I'm here to see your school, and I'll go along with that. But you can cut out the comparisons. Tindall's is run as it should be. Gateway, as far as I can gather, could do with more help. If we agree on that, maybe we can get on with looking round objectively.'

Ros made a sheepish apology. 'OK. Sorry. Our worlds are such poles apart that I can't help being constantly aware of the contrast.'

'It's not an ideal world,' he said, and the

impartial conducted tour began.

The school was quiet as the children were either at home for the weekend or on an outing to the Cotswold Farm Park. All except one—Debra, who, Matron informed them succinctly, was in bed with 'a high temperature and a very bad temper'. The previous day's excitement accounted for the fever, and fury at missing the outing was the cause of the temper.

When Ros had taken Dan through the working part of the school they went through to the bedrooms, bright with personal possessions and pleasantly cluttered, and in her own little yellow and white painted bay they found a sorry little figure lying in bed, Dan's book closed on the covers beside her.

Debra managed a pathetic attempt at a smile when she saw them.

'I was going to write to you today,' she told Dan, 'but *they* wouldn't let me. They said I had to stay here and get some boring old rest. They wouldn't let me go on the outing either, and everybody else has gone.' Her eyes glittered with threatening tears.

Dan sat on the bed. 'That's tough. I'd hate it, too. Will there be another chance.?'

'Not bloody likely! Not now that everyone else has been.'

'Debra!' Ros concealed her amusement. 'We'll say that was the fever talking, I think. And don't despair. I'll see what I can do about the outing—and that's a promise.'

Debra gave a real grin. 'Thanks, Ros.' She

looked at Dan. 'I really wanted to write and thank you for the book. Now it looks as though I'm saying it because you're here.'

'You can write to me anyway. Tell me how you feel. I'd like that.'

'Would you? It's a great book. I tried to read some just now, but my eyes are too tired.'

'Want me to read a bit for you? If Ros doesn't mind hanging around a bit.' He looked questioningly at Ros, and she suddenly realised that she had been standing there with a foolish smile on her face, watching him be so nice to the child.

'That's fine. I'll go and see Alan,' she said hurriedly, and left them to it.

Alan cut out the motor and jumped down as she walked across the grass to him.

'What goes on?' he asked. 'I wasn't expecting to see you until your day next week. And why is the party heart-throb doing the grand tour?'

'The party heart-throb turns out to be the new owner of the Dower House and half a dozen or more thriving companies,' Ros told him. 'The reason he's here is a bit complicated . . .' and you could say that again! she thought ironically. 'Basically—he seems to have more money than he knows what to do with. I thought it would be good for him to see somewhere to channel a bit of it, if he feels so inclined. Somewhere at the other end of the scale from his factories and plush offices and luxury hotels. Alan—I know you told me to keep quiet about the threat of closure, but a bit of an indiscretion—in strictest confidence, of course? Wouldn't it be in a good cause?'

Alan looked at her for a moment, then grinned. 'I didn't hear that. If any indiscretion occurs, I don't know a thing about it.' He paused for a moment, then added, more seriously, 'But it isn't just money. The lease on this land's running out. The council, I think, hankers after building something more profitable if the school's transferred. It's a big miracle you're hoping for, Ros.'

'I need one for myself, too.' She told Alan about Max's will. 'If Dan Maxton felt inclined to move Gateway into the Dower House and forget about the Stables, that would solve all our problems, wouldn't it?'

'Now you're into the realm of fantasy. And there'd still be one problem left—wouldn't there?—of a more personal nature. But I guess it's too early to ask you about that?' His eyes read her feelings. 'Yes, I see it is.' He climbed back on the mower. 'All power to your persuasive charms, Ros, but don't count on it too much. See you Tuesday.'

Ros paused outside the bedroom, watching Dan and Debra through the oval of glass in the door.

Dan was leaning against the bedhead, solemnly reading, and Debra, one hand clutching the sleeve of his sweater as though to anchor him there, had her head turned towards him and appeared to be paying rapt attention. As Ros quietly opened the door, Dan looked up at her, then down at the motionless head on the pillow.

He grinned and put his finger to his lips, then, gently disengaging Debra's fingers, he tucked her hand under the clothes and put the book on the locker beside the bed.

'If I ever wanted proof of what a boring reader I am, that's it!' he said to Ros when they were safely out of the room.

'I don't think so. Sleep is what she needs—though she'll be furious when she finds it tricked her of you. You've definitely made a conquest there.'

He slanted a humorous look at her. 'It does sometimes happen, though you may find that hard to believe from your prejudiced position.'

When they were in the car she asked him, 'Well? What did you think?'

He turned round in his seat so that he could look at her.

'It's a good place you've got there, in spite of the obvious deficiencies like physio equipment that could do with being updated. I was impressed by it. You don't have to convince me that it's doing a good job. I saw the kids at your place, remember. They were confident, full of fun . . . even Debra, at her vulnerable stage. Something about the place and the people who run it is responsible for that.'

'The equipment doesn't matter overmuch. What does is the fact that they're talking of maybe closing the school. And all because money's scarce and the land it's on could be producing more profitable returns.' Ros held her breath.

'They can't do that! It's madness! What on earth——' He broke off suddenly, and Ros looked at him in time to see his eyes harden and awareness dawn on his face. 'Wait a minute . . . and you thought how convenient all round it would be if my ideas for the Dower House underwent a metamorphosis and came out looking like a fairy-story with a happy ending for almost everybody—excluding me, of course. Is that it?'

Ros was suddenly aware of her presumptuousness and backed down.

'You said it—I didn't.'

'You didn't need to say it. It stuck out like a sore thumb.'

'People like you do sometimes step out of line and act as benefactors or whatever you like to call it.'

'And more people like you than would appear possible try to nudge them in that direction. The number of begging letters I've received in my time beggars belief.'

The scorn in his voice did away with any hope, and Ros wanted to lash out at him.

'I don't suppose you find the effort of flinging them into the bin too painful,' she said hotly. 'Not as painful as seeing yourself not pursuing profit for once.'

His face darkened. 'What I do or don't do with my profits is my concern and no one else's. And if your narrow little puritan soul wants a reputable defence of good handling of finance, try looking in the Bible. The parable of the talents doesn't exactly run down the art of making money work. But right now you're going to listen to a rational—not a hysterical—reason for your little scheme being a non-starter.'

Ros had turned stiffly away to stare out of the car window, but now he put his hand on her head in no gentle manner and forcefully twisted her round to face him.

'You've shown me a school specially constructed for special children. A school with wide doorways and ramps that wheelchairs can cope with. A school all on one floor so that everybody can go everywhere. Now think of the Dower House. Think of the doors, think of the stairs. Imagine how it would have to be ripped apart to make it even a poor second to the building that already exists. Think of the hall with that wonderful panelling and ceiling—and decide where you'd destroy both to make way for a hideous but necessary lift. Think of the darkness of the place with those diamond-paned windows—and picture children in there after the brightness of Gateway. Ask yourself whether you'd be able to bear seeing the walls knocked around and modern windows put in. Then, if you decide you're enough of a spoiler to do all that, be prepared to be turned down flat by the planning committee for suggesting such radical alterations to a listed building. Don't try to interfere with matters you know nothing about, Ros. Your efforts can be more fruitfully directed.'

He switched on the engine and the Bentley leapt forward, while Ros sat in humiliated silence, feeling lower than the road they were burning up.

Eventually, seeing that the road was unfamiliar, she said timidly, 'This isn't the way.'

'It's the way I want to go.' His voice was still tight with scorn. 'You're going to spend a further half-hour of your time looking at something you *are* qualified to express an opinion about.'

There was no trace in him now of the man who had chatted so easily with Debra. It was no good being deluded by momentary aberrations like that. There was no heart in this man—only a calculating machine.

At the other side of town, in a district that she didn't know well and which was largely rural, he turned into a lane and eventually into the forecourt of a newish house.

'I'll come straight to the point,' he said briskly. 'The last owner of this place was a fitness freak. He had a games-room built large enough to accommodate a badminton court and a table-tennis table. It would divide very easily into workshops half as big again as those you use now. And the property's in excellent shape. Only fifteen years old.' He came round to her side of the car and opened the door. 'It could be yours. You only have to say the word.'

Ros got out, seething with impotent resentment. She followed him round the house and outbuildings in stony silence, a feeling of pressure and panic building up in her. He was so pig-headedly determined . . . so set on getting his own way about the Stables. And the more he worked on her, the more unsure of herself and irrationally frightened she became.

You only have to say 'no', she told herself. He can't make you do anything you don't want to do. You're in the secure seat. The trouble was, it felt more like the tight spot.

When he finally came to a halt in the hall of the house and turned to her with a brusque 'Anything to say?' her anxiety spilled out in an uncontrolled torrent of words.

'Why won't you leave me alone? Why do you have to persist in this persecution? Can't you see that I love the Stables? Haven't you got *enough*?' She was almost crying with outrage, and she dashed a hand furiously across her eyes. 'And now you see you've reduced me to this state of idiocy—I suppose you think I've reached breaking point and any minute now I'll be giving in. But I won't, Dan Maxton. Damn you! I'll fight you every inch of the way. So you can put that in your computer and calculate how much it's going to cost you.'

She expected to see anger suffuse his face again, but instead he was looking at her in a way that took the steam out of her, and when he spoke it was quietly and reasonably.

'Ros—I'm only trying to look after your interests.'

'No, you're not!' she burst out passionately again. 'You're trying to get your own way.'

'I want to do what I think is the best thing for the property, yes. I don't deny that. The ability to see a good business prospect and the urge to see it realised is very strong in me. But you must see, in your more rational moments, that a place like this . . . all yours . . . access unrestricted——'

'Don't keep on about access! If you were so concerned, you could *give* me access to the place I really want. So that argument won't wash.'

'Perhaps I'm not foolish enough to give in over the one thing that might make you see sense. The Stables are old, Ros. The house needs a fortune spent on it. There's no central heating. There could be every kind of wood rot—the valuation will reveal that. And here's this almost new, sound building, ideal for your purposes——'

'You sound just like my father!' she said bitterly. 'He always failed to understand why people didn't jump at something better—"better" in quotes, because it never seemed better to me. You money-chasers are so horribly blinkered. The Stables is the first place to be really mine. *My* home, that *I* have control over. The last thing I want is for someone to be trying to make me move on yet again.'

She was trembling with the strength of her feelings, and he reached out suddenly and took her hands in his.

'Look at you—shaking like an aspen. Do I really have that effect on you? Ros . . .' His eyes were warm again as he looked at her. 'I don't understand what makes you this way—there's more to it than you've told me, I'm sure. But I certainly don't want to upset you like this. I'm an impatient man when I see something I want, but nothing is worth so much unhappiness. I propose we forget the Stables.'

She looked disbelievingly at him. 'Forget them for good?'

He gave her hands a little shake and smiled at her. 'That's a bit too optimistic. Not quite that. Forget them for the moment. Take time out to deal with something equally important: this phobia of yours about money. You seem unable to accept that it can be good. It can mean pleasure, you know. Wonderful experiences.'

'Not in my life. The pursuit of it meant nothing but destruction.'

'So now you generalise from that one bad experience. Won't you let me try to show you otherwise? It's poisoning you, Ros.'

She drew her hands away from his and clasped them behind her back, feeling again that power, that persuasive force flowing into herself from him. 'It's irrelevant. The thing we have to deal with is this impasse over the Stables.'

'And isn't your attitude, based on past experience, colouring your handling of the situation? Your whole attitude to life, for that matter. Can't you see? Do you really think security is in bricks and mortar, Ros? Shouldn't it come from somewhere inside you? Somewhere which only seems to contain pain and bad memories in your case. I'd like to see that change.'

She hesitated, feeling herself weakening under his persuasion. He seized the advantage. 'Give me a day. One day to try and show you the pleasure you deny yourself.' His voice was carrying her on a wave of enthusiasm. 'When are you free next week?'

'I'm at school on Tuesday and Thursday, but——'

'No buts.' He was thinking rapidly. 'Who's your favourite painter?'

She stared at him, bemused. 'My favourite . . .? Any of the Impressionists, I suppose. But I don't——'

'You're "butting" again. Right. Leave it with me. Keep Wednesday free. I'll mull over what kind of a day it's going to be, then I'll let you know the arrangements.'

He was doing it again . . . carrying her with him on the flood of this powerful determination of his, and she seemed incapable of effective resistance.

'You're going to *enjoy* yourself. For heaven's sake, don't look like that!' He ran a finger gently along the line of her lashes, smoothing away a tear that was still hanging there. Then, with a sudden smothered exclamation, he pulled her towards him and kissed her closed eyelids.

Ros told herself as he held her, one hand warm and strong on the nape of her neck, cradling her head on his shoulder, that she should be outraged again. But she wasn't. She was strangely comforted—and not just that. With the warmth and gentleness of his kiss sealing her eyes, she was waiting, every nerve vibrant with the sense of promise awakened in her by this strange man's touch.

But nothing happened, and after a moment she fought back the imprisoning waves of languor and opened her eyes to find that he was looking at her. Reading her very soul, it seemed, as the feeling of comfort began to disintegrate, to tremble into something more powerful and compelling that quickened her breathing and speeded her heartbeat. His eyes went to her parted lips, and slowly—so slowly, it seemed—his mouth closed on hers.

Only for a tantalising, blood-racing moment,

though, then he was putting her away from him, smiling as she blinked.

'And that, my little puritan, is a seal on our bargain. For the present—our truce time—there are no buyers. No sellers. Just two people in search of a better understanding of life.'

Ros swallowed hard and tore her eyes away from his, brushing an imaginary speck from her sleeve in an attempt to regain her cool.

'I don't know why I'm agreeing to all this. It's the very last thing I meant to do.'

He opened the door and motioned her through.

'I guess . . .' he said, and his voice had a faint note of surprise in it, 'I guess you could apply that to both of us. So let's not question it. Let's just get on and do it.'

CHAPTER FIVE

THE valuers came to look over the Stables early the following week, one on Monday, and the second on Tuesday when Ros got back from school. Both confirmed with maddening accuracy what Dan had predicted. All the snags he had foreseen in the property were there, and both evaluations were close enough to each other to be absolutely convincing. There was no doubt that on the market the Stables were worth less than half the property Dan had shown her and which she had so firmly turned down.

On the emotional front, Tuesday had not been an easy day. True to her promise, Ros had given Alan the most honest answer she could to his proposal without being downright cruel. It was something lacking in herself, she assured him, because there was no fault to be found in him. But the fact remained that she was afraid she didn't feel for him as she thought one ought to feel about a prospective husband.

'Of course you don't. You haven't had the chance to get to that point,' Alan told her reasonably. 'I went about it badly, Ros. Rushed at you like the proverbial bull in the china shop. Let's stay friends. Leave the options open and see what develops.'

She hadn't felt able to refuse his modest request.

But she knew it wouldn't work. Alan was so good, so
kind, so admirable—all the positive adjectives you
could possibly trot out. But he didn't have the power
to rouse her as she knew she could be roused. Dan
Maxton had underlined that point for her. He was
not admirable. His philosophy of life couldn't be
more different from hers. But if she could feel as she
did at the kiss of a man like him, then somewhere
there had to be the right sort of man with the right
sort of chemistry. Nothing was going to make her
settle for less.

Tammy and Paul, when not working, were
spending more time away without saying what they
were doing. A divide seemed to be opening up
between the three of them, leaving Ros isolated on
one side of it. It wasn't that anyone actually put it
into words. In fact, too little was said on any subject,
and Ros was as guilty of silence as anyone. She had
told them nothing about Wednesday's mystery
outing with Dan. Tammy had asked about his visit
to Gateway, but only hurriedly, and for reasons of
her own Ros had not gone on to speak of the house
she had been offered.

For the same reasons, she kept the result of the
valuations to herself. She didn't want their 'told you
so' looks. She had enough pressure from Dan—at
least, she *had* had enough pressure from him until
this crazy truce that he had initiated, and about
which she now had decidedly cold feet.

He had phoned once on Monday, his voice cool
and brisk, to ask if she had a passport. Since then she
had heard nothing, and by mid-way through

Tuesday evening she was almost convinced that he had written off the idea. Relief and pique tangled in her.

Then, shortly after eight, when they were all three in the kitchen still after eating, the phone rang and Ros had an inhibiting audience when she answered it.

'About tomorrow . . .' Dan began crisply. No 'Hello', no 'How are you?'. She could almost see him ticking off items on an agenda as he spoke to her. 'I'll pick you up at seven a.m. No later. Wear something comfortable. Something you can cope with all manner of transport in, and all kinds of sightseeing. There's a challenge for you. No crazy heels, for instance. But decent. Be ready for all kinds of places.'

'Is that all?' Ros asked a shade sarcastically.

'Isn't it enough?'

'A bit more specific information about the programme I'm sure you've worked out might help.'

'You'll find out what that is in due course. Don't forget your passport.'

'You do know I have to be back for school on Thursday?' she asked nervously.

'Don't worry. I didn't tell you to bring an overnight bag, did I? You'll be back in time to spend at least some of the night in your own chaste bed. So don't get worked up about nothing, Snow Queen.'

His tone stung. 'It isn't too late for either of us to change our minds,' she threatened.

'You won't. You're a word-keeper. And I've gone

too far with the organising to do anything so stupid. You're going to enjoy yourself, I told you. And it's going to be a fine day, by the way.'

'Oh. So you control the weather, too?' she retorted.

He laughed shortly. 'It sometimes feels like it. This has been one of those days when I seem to have been doing ten men's work. So the last thing I want right now is any hassle from you. See you at seven. I shall be all charm after a night's sleep. That's a promise.' The line went dead.

Ros dropped the phone back on the rest and stood frowning at it.

'What goes on?' Tammy asked.

'I wish I could tell you. Dan Maxton wants me to go off with him tomorrow, but he won't say where.' She strove for light-heartedness, but felt far from it. 'If I don't come back, try looking abroad for me. All I know is that I need a passport.'

'Surprising what you have to do to sort out a property deal,' Paul said laconically.

'If I wanted to sort out any kind of deal, I could do it like that!' Ros snapped her fingers. 'It's sticking to the idea of not selling that causes the trouble.'

Paul and Tammy exchanged glances, then as though by a prearranged plan, they got up and began to clear the dishes.

The switch-off again, Ros thought crossly.

'All right! Clam up, then,' she said. She had cooked the meal, so clearing up wasn't her province. She poured herself a large coffee from the pot on the stove and made for the stairs to sort out what on earth she could wear next day to fit in with Dan's instructions. The last thing she must do, she thought sarcastically, was fail to come up to his expectations.

Paul came after her and gripped her arm, making her slop coffee into the saucer.

'It *is* your problem, Ros, you know. We really can't do anything about it but stand back and let you make your decision.'

She pulled a face. 'I know. But nothing seems the same, does it? I wish we could put the clock back. Have Max still here, and no problems at all.'

Paul took her cup and tipped the spilled coffee back into it.

'You'll come to the right decision in your own good time. And if I seem preoccupied, or Tammy does, well—we've maybe got one or two problems of our own. But they'll pass, like yours. So perish the lot of 'em, eh?'

Ros grinned at him, suddenly cheered.

'Elegantly put. I'll go along with that sentiment.'

With one of the sudden mood reversals that seemed to be her lot these days, Ros began to feel quite a little zip of anticipatory excitement about the next day. Whatever else could be said about Dan Maxton, life in his orbit certainly was not dull.

She had solved the clothes question rather well, she told herself while she waited by the window, watching the courtyard for Dan's car.

She was wearing black trousers and an open-knit black summer sweater with a swathe of tiny bright turquoise beads and matching ear-rings. Her roomy leather shoulder-bag was the same colour as the beads, and the black patent ballet pumps would take her right through the day in comfort and still look dainty enough for evening wear. The trousers passed for cotton, but they were actually beautifully cut in dull silk crêpe de Chine, and in her bag was a tiny matching shoestring-strapped camisole top. Also folded away in the bag was a dazzling silk evening jacket that had all the blues and greens of a peacock's tail in it, bits of the pattern outlined in fine gold thread. Ros knew from experience that it would come out of the bag looking as fresh and uncrushed as a newly ironed garment. That change effected, and with her blue costume jewellery replaced by the gold chain and gold tassel ear-rings she had with her, she felt equal to any evening entertainment Dan might like to spring on her.

Daks was fed and had gone back into his basket, aware by dog's radar that he was not included in the day, but he pricked up his ears at the sound of the car engine.

'Don't get out, boy. It isn't worth it,' Ros told him. 'Tammy's going to feed you, and I expect you'll get Paul to take you for a walk.' His baleful eyes watched her over the side of the basket as she closed the kitchen door behind her.

'Good morning!' Dan called, getting out and coming round to open the door for her. 'You have a singularly small amount of luggage, I must say.'

'All I need, to the best of my knowledge,' Ros said, sliding into the front seat and dropping her bag down at her feet. 'Don't blame me if your own secrecy has its pitfalls.'

'I wanted to surprise you.'

'You're constantly doing that.'

They looked at each other and laughed, then Dan reached for her hand and brought her fingers up to his lips for a brief kiss.

'Well, here's to a day of pleasant surprises.'

The engine purred into powerful life and the car began to devour the sparkling, early-morning lanes and roads.

'No clues?' Ros asked.

'Just one. The first change of transport comes at the airport.'

She had been prepared for that. A single day abroad called for the fastest means of getting there. What Ros was not prepared for when they went through Customs was to be led towards a trim blue and white Cessna 421. As the two smiling, smart crew helped her into the passenger section of the private plane, she noticed Dan's company logo painted on the gleaming bodywork.

Inside, though she had to stoop a little and Dan rather a lot, once they were settled in the luxurious club-style seats the plane was extremely comfortable.

'Not scared, I hope?' Dan asked, glancing sideways as the engine surged up to full roar.

'Just a bit. I've only flown once before, and that was in a monster where we were packed like sardines.'

'You'll like this much better. You feel you belong to the sky much more in a small plane. Not so much of an intruder.'

He saw her tense as they gathered speed on the runway, and she found that her hand was being comfortably gripped by his, and that she was glad to have a warm, human response to her convulsive clutching.

The take-off was much more pleasant than her previous experience, and she quickly relaxed, but when she tried casually to remove her hand from his, Dan said, 'Leave it where it is. I've just got used to it.' Ros darted a quick look at him, and he added, 'Told you I'd be all charm today, didn't I? See if you recognise anything down below.'

Her attention diverted to the toytown fields and villages below them, Ros sat quite contentedly watching the unfolding landscape.

'France?' she asked, when the sparkling water of the Channel gave way to land again.

'Yes, France,' he said, adding infuriatingly, 'But it's a big place, the field's still wide open.'

They landed at a small private airfield, and Ros had no chance to find out where they were.

A hired car was waiting, and one of the crew who had flown them over changed roles and drove them along tree-lined roads and eventually through a little town whose roads were shaded by lime trees, and whose name, she managed to see this time, was Vernon. When they had left the last building behind the car slowed and coasted to a halt on grassy rough ground at the roadside.

'Any wiser yet?' Dan asked, his dark eyes teasing.

'Not really,' she said. They were parked near the

river, she could see now that she had got out. Dan had a quick, cryptic word with the driver, checking that he knew where he was to meet them, then he made for the water's edge where a rowing-boat was moored.

'Goodness! Are we going in that now?' she couldn't help exclaiming. 'Is the day going to be non-stop travelling? When do we get down to a couple of donkeys?' Dan smiled knowingly but didn't answer, just helped her into the boat.

'You said you liked water, and this really is the best way to go . . . to the place we're going to,' he said maddeningly.

'It's the Seine,' she guessed, dabbling a hand in the water.

'Right. But not for long. We need to go against the current, so I shall be pulling into a tributary where it'll be easier going.' He was taking off his sweater as he spoke, revealing strong, suntanned arms, well-muscled below the sleeves of the plain white sweatshirt he was wearing.

He began to pull on the oars, and Ros thought that he looked as much at home and as absolutely right in this little boat as he did in his plane or at the bedside of an out-of-sorts ten-year-old.

'Why not a slinky power-boat?' she asked suddenly.

'And spoil the atmosphere?' he replied with feeling, then added with a grin, 'And there are tree stumps it's as well to encounter at slow speed.' He was quiet for a while, then he said, 'Well? What do you think?'

Ros, who had been watching him again, hypnotised by the regular rhythm of the oars, jumped and blushed at his words.

He smiled. 'About the river, not me. You're supposed to be a water freak, you tell me.'

'It's beautiful,' she told him with feeling. They were in the tributary now, and the close-wooded shores made a leafy green tunnel, roofed by a sparkling, cloudless sky. The only sound was the gentle, regular plunking splash of the oars.

They had moored the boat and made their way across a field towards a village before Ros realised in a flash where she was going.

'Giverny!' she cried when she saw the place name at the side of the road they had come out on. 'Monet's house, that's it, isn't it? The water garden. That's where you're taking me. That's why you asked me about my favourite artist. Well!' She looked up at him with grudging admiration. 'I never dreamed of this. To see the originals of all those wonderful water-lily paintings . . . How could you have thought up anything so marvellous?'

'That's the idea of the day, isn't it?'

'But I never thought . . . I mean, I half expected you to——'

'To take you to some gallery or other and buy a picture? You can put money to far more imaginative use than that.'

The house, which Claude Monet, the leader of the Impressionists, had bought and so lovingly turned into a place of beauty, and whose garden was immortalised in the series of vast canvases of water-lily studies known the world over, nestled against a hillside, its garden a blaze of colour. The flowers were massed and scattered broadcast, not regimented, with stunning effect, and the path to the door was spanned by trellised arches heavy with roses.

But it was the water garden across the road that Ros couldn't wait to see, and when she stood eventually at the side of the lake she felt she could gaze for ever. The lilies were crimson, pink, cream, white and lemon, sculptured petals unfolding above olive-green fleshy leaves. They grew in floating islands, and between the islands the surface of the water was a constantly changing mirror of the sky above and the willows that trailed and dipped their leaves in its surface.

'Explain to me what it was about this pool that fascinated Monet so much,' Dan said, breaking the silence.

'Who am I to attempt to explain? But I think it was the fact that it seems to live. Dark sometimes, sometimes dazzling. Sometimes disturbed by the movement of reflected clouds. Never the same. And against such a living background, the statuesque beauty of the lilies. He tried again and again to capture it, you know that, of course. But always it was changing, offering something new.' She tore her eyes from the water and looked at Dan. 'A Chinese artist once said "If your subject is a pear tree, it is not a pear tree you have to paint; you must paint the dance of the soul of a pear tree." I think Monet was doing something like that. Painting his experience of the soul of a lake. O-o-o-h!'

She flung out her arms, then ran suddenly up on to the arched bridge that spanned the lake. At the top of the arch she stopped and leaned on the side, heavy, luxurious trails of wistaria over her head and under her arms.

'Never in my wildest dreams did I imagine I'd one day stand on this bridge that I've seen in so many of Monet's paintings, looking at all this. It's the experience of a lifetime, Dan. Thank you.'

He looked at the glowing face in its frame of purple and green.

'If I were your Chinese painter with a gift for words, I'd say that the best way to paint something lovely would be to catch it reflected in the face of a beautiful onlooker.'

His eyes held hers for a moment, then he walked up to join her on the bridge and she watched him coming towards her, unable to move, unable to take her eyes from him.

When he reached her, the world seemed to fall silent. Ros could feel herself being drawn by a powerful, invisible magnetism, closer and closer to him, though he was not touching her.

'What—what are you doing?' she asked breathlessly, her inept words an attempt to break free of the incomprehensible sense of possession.

He bent his head and kissed her on the lips, still not touching her with his hands, only the warm compulsion of his mouth on hers holding her spellbound.

'I'm paying my own tribute to beauty,' he said,

and his words seemed to set her free. She had a sudden overflowing feeling of happiness, and it was she who took the initiative, flinging her arms round his neck, pressing her body against his and her lips again to his mouth. She was a riot of sensations, all her senses feeing the exhilaration that was in her. The beauty of the place, the strength of the experience intoxicated her, and it was right that such happiness should overflow and be shared with the man who had made it possible, who had devised the very happening that would speak so powerfully to her.

'Thank you, Dan,' she said eventually again, and heaved a huge sigh of happiness.

He had knotted his pullover round his shoulders, but Ros had dislodged it, and as he reached to retrieve it from the handrail of the bridge where it had fallen, he said wryly, 'Was that what it was all about, then? A kiss of thanks?'

Ros was still on a high. 'It was a kiss because a kiss was necessary. *Right* at that point.'

He looked at her, his eyes scanning her face, her glowing blue eyes, her shining hair.

'You funny little thing!' he said, giving her slim shoulders a hug as they came down from the bridge and walked round the clustered reeds and bullrushes backed by bamboo and ancient weeping willows.

When Ros eventually managed to indicate that she could tear herself away from the garden, he said, 'I'm going to depart from my original plan, I think. I had intended to take you to see the water-lily paintings in Paris, but for today I think you might prefer to hang on to the reality rather than the representation. In a way, keep closer to Monet's dream.'

Ros was surprised by his sensitivity. 'I think you're right,' she said slowly, because it was a big temptation. 'I'd love to see the paintings, but for a little while I want to keep the memory of the garden.'

'Only the garden?' he asked softly.

The memory of his body, lean and hard and powerful against hers, brought the colour to her cheeks.

He laughed. 'All right. Come on, water nymph. We can come back for the paintings another day.'

The car was outside the gates, and Dan gave rapid instructions to the driver. Soon they were parking again and entering a cool old *auberge* with stone floors and thick uneven walls washed white.

'If you'd like to refresh yourself, I'll rearrange our schedule and meet you on the terrace. The table's booked. Just mention my name on your way through,' Dan told her.

The magic of the morning extended through the lunch hour. The meal was a fantasy of flavour and a delight to the eye. They had duck liver *millefeuille*, light and melting with its contrastingly crisp garnish of fine slivers of celery and apple. Then came salmon poached with asparagus, and, when Ros thought she could not eat another thing, she was offered mouthwatering pineapple fritters *à la pina colada*, and capitulated instantly.

'We're still going to Paris,' Dan said as the car

whisked them away again.

Ros was swept breathlessly to the top of the Eiffel Tower. She was led along arcades dazzling with exotic window displays of jewellery and clothes. She was taken round the cool, vaulted interior of Notre-Dame, where she walked through pools of vivid colours thrown on the stone floor by the wonderful stained-glass windows.

They had tea on the terrace of a café on the Champs Elysées while her mind replayed the kaleidoscope of images over and over to her.

Dan smiled understandingly. 'And now you need a restful hour or so. I have a room reserved for your use at a little hotel nearby. You can have a bath . . . call in a hairdresser, if you like—one's alerted . . . or just go to sleep for a while. Then at seven we go to a private fashion show I've arranged at a designer's called Ottilie Kleber in the Forum des Halles.'

'How can we do that?' Ros struggled out of her daydream. 'If there's no intention of buying, how can we possibly go and watch dresses being paraded under false pretences?'

Dan's eyes widened in amused mockery. 'But we can do anything, my little puritan. Money opens all doors—and if we don't buy anything today, they'll shrug and think we may do so later.'

'You're not going to try and embarrass me?' Ros said anxiously. 'I wouldn't stand for that, you know.'

'Would I do that? Why do you think I'm telling you in advance? I want you to be quite relaxed and enjoy the show without any fear of awkwardness.

After that we'll go and eat at a very special place, and I'll show you a bit of Paris by night. Then maybe we'll have to think about going home.'

The words aroused a pang of unwilling protest in Ros. She wanted this day to last for ever. She was spellbound by it. Totally bewitched, bewildered and bedazzled by it. The word 'maybe' echoed in her mind. Surely Dan wasn't going to turn awkward after all the wonderful things they'd done?

And if he did, so what? She could cope with it. It wouldn't be the first time she'd had to call a halt. She wasn't going to spoil this lovely day by worrying about a possibly troublesome end to it.

She was glad to use the luxurious facilities of the room reserved in her name and soak in a scented bath with every kind of toiletry there at hand for her. She didn't call in the hairdresser. That would have seemed too personal a charge on Dan's bank account, and besides, there was everything necessary for dealing with her own hair—something she was no stranger to doing.

She was completely revived by the thoughtful little oasis of quiet in the hectic day, and when she opened the door to Dan's knock Ros felt ready for anything.

He had changed into a fresh silk shirt and tie, and put on the jacket of his suit. It wasn't enough of a change to make her feel awkward if she had worn what she had been wearing for the earlier part of the day, but enough to emphasise the lean elegance of his tall figure.

He walked round her without speaking, taking in the upswept hair, the glowing colours of the silk jacket, the gleam of gold against her skin, itself flushed with gold after the day in the sun.

'Well—I didn't plan all this, did I?' he said. 'How you managed it, I don't know, but you look lovely, Ros. The whole thing is a triumph of ingenuity.'

She was attempting to crush her jumper into her shoulder-bag.

'This gives the game away,' she said. 'Unfortunately it's more bulky than the jacket and top.'

Dan took the jumper from her and tossed it over on to the bed.

'Leave it. While we're eating. Mark's going to come back and collect our bits and pieces from here. No need to spoil yourself with a bulging bag. Shall we go?'

The velvet and gold and crystal of Ottilie Kleber's showrooms would have daunted Ros, but with Dan at her side, urbane, self-assured, and obviously familiar with the *patronne*, she accepted her little gold and midnight-blue velvet chair with aplomb and caught a fleeting, satisfying glimpse of her own reflection in the gilt-framed mirrors that surrounded the room before giving her full attention to the parade of beautiful clothes that was beginning.

The Kleber genius was to use fabrics reminiscent of past centuries, but in a way that was thoroughly modern. Laces and velvets, silk, tulle, satin, brocade—all were used in brilliant combination, sewn with beads, embroidered, and dyed in antique, subtle shades of gold and rose and aqua and cream, a patchwork of textures and colours that took the breath away.

Ros was invited to finger the fabrics as the models swayed and postured, directing their smiles and striking their poses for her alone, and at the end of the parade she turned a radiant face to Dan.

'If only Tammy could have seen all that! She'd have been over the moon. What incredibly beautiful clothes they were.'

She turned again to her especial favourite—a calf-length dress in shades of muted rose that had appealed particularly because it was simpler than the rest, somehow more accessible than the more exotic models, though it was foolish to think of any of these fairy-like garments as being available to someone like her.

True to Dan's promise, there was no embarrassment. Both models and *patronne* smilingly thanked them for coming to see the show, and Ros carried the memory of the rainbow beauty of the clothes with her as they drove to the restaurant—Robuchon's, in the rue de Longchamps.

There they were shown to a secluded table, separated from the rest as all the tables were by wood-framed glass screens. The light from lamps, flattering and intimate, fell on pink walls, beige napery, flowered chintz and plinths on which stood huge white *faïence* vases holding a riot of fresh flowers.

'You'll get a kind of picture show here, after all,' Dan said as they read the menus. 'You'll find that the food is an artistic creation in its own right on the plate—*nouvelle cuisine* at its most magnificent.'

Champagne sparkled in their glasses, and added zest and light-heartedness to their conversation throughout the meal. Lobster with saffron pasta was followed by rack of lamb with breadcrumbed truffles, each course served and displayed on the plate with loving artistry. A delicious *crème brûlée* rounded off the meal, and a glass of old cognac set the seal of excellence.

Ros wondered what Dan could possibly have planned as a suitable end to the day after such a surfeit of enjoyment. The car took them to the Latin Quarter, not to a glamorous nightclub as she had half expected, but to a little square where there were tables under the plane trees and tiny white lights like stars against the dark velvet of the sky threaded in the branches. A little accordion group was playing for dancing in the open air. It was so French, so beautiful, and so right an end to the day.

With the sound of the accordions lilting and swelling, Ros slipped into Dan's arms and he held her close as they danced in and out of the shadows, now fast and breathlessly as the music dictated, now slowly and dreamily, with the stars and the twinkling lights and the gently moving leaves weaving magic overhead.

Time ceased to exist until Ros found herself being danced to the fringe of the crowd and away into a shady alley, at the far end of which she could see the Seine sparkling in the moonlight.

'Time to go,' Dan said reluctantly as the music faded away into the distance and their dancing slowed to a halt. But his arms still held her and his voice was soft persuasion in her ear. 'Think of those rooms in the hotel. You only have to say the word and we could stay on . . . dance longer—as long as you like . . .'

And share one room at the end of it, no doubt. Ros's senses were blurring under the seduction of his voice and his touch. It would have seemed so right for them to stay together, to end this wonderful day in each other's arms. She wanted that . . . but she was bewitched. She had to remember that. This wasn't real. It was a period of enchantment, a day out of life's normal pattern. Morning would come, and sanity, and self-recrimination.

'I've got to get back,' she said with difficulty. Then, with an attempt at lightness, but an attempt betrayed by the catch in her voice, she added, 'Everything turns to dust and ashes at midnight in the enchanted kingdom, remember. Let's not be around for that to happen.'

His eyes searched her face in the moonlight, then he shrugged and made a little wry face of resignation. 'I'd be less than a man if I hadn't at least tried . . . Come on, then, my little puritan. Your glass coach awaits.'

He laced his fingers in hers and they walked to the end of the alley and along beside the Seine as far as the next bridge, where the car was waiting. Ros was both glad and sorry to be back in a safe threesome with the patient Mark. She had come so close, so very close, to losing her head back there.

The car sped through the silent night towards the

airfield, but it was the comfortable silence of companionship, not, Ros was sleepily aware, a silence spiked with resentment. She had to hand it to Dan for that, and she was thankful to be able to do so. It would have spoiled everything if he had been angry.

They settled in the plane while Mark handed over the keys of the hired car, then the plane taxied forward into the darkness.

'Enjoy your day?' Dan asked.

Ros sighed. 'How could I do otherwise? It was wonderful.'

'I proved my point?'

'You know you did.'

'Then here's something for you.' He reached down beside his seat and lifted up a purple and silver bag with Ottilie Kleber's sloping black signature across it. 'I know you liked this one best. It showed on your face. You can't hide what you're feeling, can you, Ros?'

Ros knew what the bag contained before she opened it. In silence she looked at the folds of rose silk and velvet and brocade. She wanted it. She really wanted it. But at the same time she could feel her own words coming true. The day *was* turning to dust and ashes, because experiences to treasure were one thing, a dress that must have cost hundreds of pounds was suspiciously like an attempt to buy her. She cursed his wealth and his knowingness and his oh, so discerning eye. She was not for sale. She had seen enough of buying.

'If my feelings are so self-evident, you must see

what I am feeling now, Dan,' she said quietly. 'I
can't accept a gift like this from you. The day and all
it held—for that I thank you. But I won't have a
concrete reminder of what I owe you. You're going
to have to send this back. I'm sorry.'

The atmosphere was suddenly electric.

'You can't be serious!' His voice sliced through
the air and she felt herself flinch.

'I'm *absolutely* serious.' She smarted with the
injustice of being put in this position. 'And now, I
suppose, because I won't sit back and be bought, the
magic's over. That's sad. Really sad.'

'You think it's so important to me? That a few
bloody rags mean anything at all?' They were
airborne now and he leaned forward and clicked on
the intercom with the cockpit. 'Mark? Come
through when you've a minute, will you?' He
turned back to Ros, and though he masked it with a
smile that didn't reach his eyes, she felt the strength
of his resentment. 'We'll soon dispose of that little
misconception of yours.'

Mark stepped through into the passenger section.

'Anything wrong, Mr Maxton?'

'Wrong? Hell, no! Catch this.' He flung the
couturier's bag across and Mark, though taken by
surprise, still managed to catch it. 'Give this to your
wife—it's a bit of nonsense she may appreciate. We
find it's the wrong size for Miss Howard. Isn't that a
pity? If it doesn't fit your wife, tell her to pass it on.
Oh—and tell her not to read too much into it! It's
just a souvenir from abroad.'

Mark looked embarrassed. 'Are you sure, Mr

Maxton? Clothes aren't my strong point, but this looks pretty posh to me.'

'It's pretty. That's the relevant word. Get back in there now, and I hope she likes it.'

When Mark had rejoined his co-pilot, Dan folded his arms and slid down comfortably in his seat. 'That's that, then,' he said.

Ros felt humiliated. 'You didn't have to do that.'

'Why not? It was a trifle. Just something I foolishly thought would please you. Too bad I tripped over one of your hang-ups again.'

She felt a sudden surge of aggression. 'And what about your hang-ups? What about your spend-spend-spend fixation? Why couldn't you leave well alone? Money has to come into everything.'

'Don't talk rubbish,' he said scathingly. 'Money wasn't at all what the essence of today was about. I tried to give you a day beyond money, but which money made more accessible. Evidently I failed to convince you of that small truth.'

Memories of all they had done flooded back to reproach her.

'No, you didn't fail,' she sighed. 'It was a very special day—up to the point of getting on the plane.' She turned to him with sudden spirit. 'But would you be willing to make yourself available to counter-persuasion? Could you believe that a special day could be had without all the resources you have at your fingertips? A day that cost nothing at all. Or would that shake the foundations of your particular world too much?'

He looked down at her, and the arrogant set of his

features softened into a reluctant grin.

'All right, Tiger. What an infuriatingly resilient woman you are. Name the day—only let it be soon.'

'Why?' she taunted. 'Is your time-out period beginning to prove a strain? Are you wanting to get back to business?'

'Think what you like. End of argument,' he said with finality. 'Now I'm going to put out the lights so that the panorama of England by night isn't wasted. I suggest you start looking and stop talking.'

With the cabin in darkness, Ros looked down at the twinkling lights below. Dan was silent, and she had plenty of time to wonder how many of the lives represented by the pinpricks of light were as strange and complicated as her own.

CHAPTER SIX

ROS thought a lot about the form the day of retalitation should take. Her final plans had dangerous dependence on good weather, but she could do nothing other than hope about that. She told Dan that she would like his company the following Monday from four o'clock in the afternoon.

'Is that the earliest day you can manage?' he asked.

'I've got orders I must work on over the weekend. Life goes on, you know,' she told him impatiently.

'And why four o'clock? Having trouble finding enough free activities to fill a day, are you?'

'It's a question of timing, not economy,' she said sharply. 'And incidentally, if the weather's not good, I'd like you to be prepared to postpone the outing to a better day.'

'What a lot of provisos seem to surround your day!' he protested.

'You were lucky. It wouldn't have been quite the same if we'd been rowing down the Seine in a rainstorm.'

'Lucky—rubbish. I'm the sort the gods smile on.'

'Then you'd better pray they smile on my day out,' she said tartly. 'I want you to promise you'll bring nothing in the way of financial back-up. No money, no cheque-book, no cashcards. Just yourself, dressed for action.'

'And what might that mean?'

'Shorts and trainers if it's fine, and if you possess such things.'

'We're going to run a marathon?'

'Wait and see. I had to, didn't I?'

She was smiling as she put the phone down. Her day would have a very salutory effect on this man with his fleet of planes and cars and boats. It would be interesting to find out how he coped with more primitive methods of locomotion.

'Paul—could I borrow your bike next Monday?' she asked at dinner that night.

'OK. But what's wrong with yours? Is it out of action?'

'No. I'll be using mine myself. Yours is for Dan Maxton.'

He laughed disbelievingly at her. 'You're joking! I shouldn't think he knows one end of a bike from the other.'

'Maybe he hasn't looked too closely at one in recent years. But every boy rides a bike at some point. He'll remember how.'

'And if you're taking him on one of your long runs, he'll know about it if he's as out of practice as that!' Tammy said. 'What's the idea now, Ros? You're leaving me way behind in this odd relationship. Put me in the picture in words of one syllable, will you? The man wants to buy your property. You don't want to sell. How does sitting him on a bike solve anything?'

Ros started to clear the table. 'It started off with the property, and we'll be getting back to that. But right now we seem stuck on trying to understand each other's world. Don't blame me. He started it, and he's the one who seems to think it has some bearing.'

'I can think of reasons for understanding each other being important,' Tammy said, her head on one side as she eyed Ros questioningly. 'But they're nothing to do with buying and selling. Ros—you're not going to get hurt at the end of all this, are you?'

'Me?' Ros flung back her hair impatiently. 'Why should I get hurt? It's a simple matter of calmly getting to know each other's viewpoints so that we can sort out a problem.'

'On a bike,' Paul added solemnly, then burst out laughing. 'Go on, Ros. You lead a sober life normally. You're entitled to a bit of summer madness. Just make sure it ends some time.'

And it is madness, Ros told herself later that night, unable to get to sleep. What was she doing? She kept getting caught up in Dan Maxton's strong, forceful personality so that whatever he suggested she eventually fell in with—and that way danger lay. She was allowing herself to be ensnared in the net that he hoped would eventually trap her. It had to stop. After Monday, no more. She would tell him, absolutely finally, that she would not sell, and put an end to these delaying tactics.

*　　*　　*

Monday was all that she could have hoped for. The sky was clear and stayed so throughout the morning and early afternoon. Ros cleaned and oiled the bikes—both ancient models, but that fitted in quite well with the point she was making.

Dan must have left his car at the Dower House, because when she stood up from a last checking of the tyres, he was there in the courtyard, dazzling in white shorts and blue and white shirt and trainers.

'Here I am, almost in a state of nature according to instructions,' he grinned, pulling the pockets of his shorts inside out to illustrate that they concealed nothing. 'Not a penny on me—nothing to sell, even, apart from my watch and I shan't part with that.' He eyed the bikes. 'Is there a vintage bike race, then? Something like the London to Brighton thing for cars?'

'Just a straightforward cycle ride,' Ros said, standing up and trying not to let her eyes wander. Dan could wear shorts as few men could, in her experience. His legs were brown and firm and long, and she was reminded again that, no matter how different their approach to life might be, physical attraction was a great remover of obstacles.

'I hope you're going to be able to cope,' she said impudently.

'Oh, I think so.' He swung his leg over Paul's bike and circled the yard competently until Daks dashed in pursuit. 'As long as this hound of yours isn't in the party!' he called, wobbling to a halt.

Her momentary awkwardness forgotten, Ros stood laughing at the pair of them, her spirits undergoing the sudden swing to high that kept overtaking her these days. She knew that she was just as likely to plummet to low if she allowed herself to think that this would be the last time she would go out with Dan, but she was determined to enjoy the day and make her point successfully.

The first stop was to be the wooded heights overlooking the chain of reservoirs, and she had made that part of the run several times between last week and now, to check that her timing was right for what she wanted Dan to see.

She found that, despite his life-style, Dan was no mean cyclist. She was the one who gave in and dismounted on the steep hill leading up to the first stop.

'I suppose you have a private gymnasium to keep you in trim?' she panted as they pushed their bikes up the last couple of hundred yards.

'No. Living in hotels and rented accommodation means that I never get the chance to make each place ideal. But I work out pretty regularly at whichever health club is near.' He cast an amused glance at her flushed face. 'You should try it.'

'You mean you have no permanent home?'

'Only in the sense that my parents' smallholding will always be a base for me. I've been so much on the move so far, and it's suited me to be able to live wherever the current work's going on and then up-roots and move when necessary with a minimum of fuss.'

'I suppose that's what you'll do when you've finished with the Dower House?' She couldn't help saying it, although the mention of his going away gave her a very odd feeling.

Dan stretched over the handlebars and laid a finger on her lips.

'You're getting suspiciously near talking shop, and that's taboo.'

They walked on in silence for a moment. 'All the same,' Ros persisted, 'I can't understand anyone being satisfied with living in hotels. My home means so much to me.'

'And so will mine. It's a question of having the right someone to make a permanent home with. For me, that comes before the place. Only it—or she—hasn't yet.'

Ros thought not too happily along those lines for a while.

'Has Karen been to see the Dower House yet?' she asked, then wished instantly that she hadn't.

'Not yet, but it's on the cards. Are you wondering if she's the one to make me settle down? What an inquisitive mood you're in!' He was laughing at her, but they were at the top of the hill, at the point where a break in the trees gave a good view down over the water.

Ros pushed her bike over to the side and rested it against a tree.

'Well, we're here now, and there may be a bit of a wait before the happening I want to show you, so you can ask a few questions yourself if you feel the need to get your own back.'

He parked his own bike and sat down on the grass beside her.

'All right. Tell me what's behind this money phobia of yours. Really behind it, I mean. Don't tell me a few changes of house caused it. I know you haven't told me the full story yet.'

His attack was so direct, so much to the roots of her, that she stared at him, her defences suddenly crumbling, the truth wanting to fight its way out of her and herself powerless to stop it.

'That's not fair,' she hedged, her fingers plucking nervously at the grass between them.

'Fair or not, I want to know. Tell me.' He captured her hand and held it still in his.

Ros took a quivering breath, then suddenly she was telling him. She was even finding a kind of relief in talking about the happenings that had so hurt her, and he was listening as though he really wanted to hear and not as though it was just something to pass the time.

'Well—you're right,' she said. 'The fact that we were constantly moving house wasn't the only thing. It was only the start of something worse. In the end, it wasn't his job or his house that my father changed, it was his wife and family—and he did it in the most brutal way. He just went off to Australia with a woman half my mother's age. There was no advance warning . . . no explanation. He didn't even think that I merited a goodbye. I was left to try and stop my mother going to pieces. Try, and fail. She had enough money—that was one of the things he did, typically, consider important enough to see to. And it was in spending money that she tried to console herself. She spent on drink, on clothes, on jewellery on odds and ends for the house . . . and none of it brought her a trace of peace of mind. She never recovered.'

'How old were you?'

'I was fourteen.'

His hand was firm, gripping hers. 'And what happened to your father?'

'He died. I never saw him again. It was the summer of the bush fires, and both of them were trapped, both he and his woman.' She gave a mirthless little laugh. 'They never married because my mother wouldn't divorce him. So all the rest of the money came back to us. Not for long, though. My mother began playing the Stock Exchange. She soon got rid of it. And so it went on. In my last term at school I was called in to the headmistress's study. My mother had died because of a stupid accident. She had fallen downstairs. They didn't have to tell me that she had been drinking. The inquest confirmed it, however.' She sighed. 'Well—there you are. A sordid little story. Do you feel it explains my attitude?'

He was silent for a moment, looking at her, his eyes dark and inscrutable. 'It explains what an unhappy childhood you had. But you attach all blame to the pursuit and possession of money. Don't you think that people, with all their weaknesses, come into it? You see your father as greedy for success—greedy for change. I wonder if he was perhaps driven by your mother to do what he did. Maybe he was living a life he didn't believe in. Maybe he stuck it for so long, then broke. Do you really know? What did he do in Australia? Did he go on in the same way there?'

'Apparently not,' she said reluctantly. 'He had a little farm, the lawyers told us. Nothing grand. The ambitious streak seemed in abeyance.'

'Or maybe he was no longer driven, and he could be content with what he had.'

'You don't know. You didn't live through it!' she said passionately.

'That's true. But ask yourself again what your mother did. Had she any inner resources beyond the attempt to comfort herself with one purchase after another? Would you have behaved as she did?'

'No. Of course I wouldn't. I'd have made some kind of life for myself.'

'Then that brings us back to human weakness again, doesn't it?'

Ros had had enough of his probing. She jumped to her feet.

'I don't know why we're talking about all this. I believe you're trying to spoil my day.'

In a flash he was standing beside her, gripping her shoulders so that it hurt. 'You little fool! You talk of spoiling your day when I'm trying to disentangle your life!'

'My life's fine.'

'Is it? *Is it*?' he stressed.

For a moment they stared at each other, blue eyes against brown, then Ros slumped, the fight gone out of her, and Dan, repentant, pulled her into an apologetic hug.

'You're right on one point,' he said. 'I shouldn't

have brought up the past right now. Here we are on top of the world. We should be looking around, not back.'

Ros let herself be held. There had never been anyone to comfort her when she needed it. Arms holding her close made something melt inside her. She could hear his heart beating strongly right there where her head rested against his chest, and it was the most reassuring sound in the world.

Then over its rhythm came the discordant sound she had been waiting for—the distant cry of the wild geese.

'Look!' she breathed, and with Dan's arms still round her they both turned to scan the sky over the water.

From beyond the hills, the V-shaped formation of more than twenty birds came winging straight as an arrow against the glowing blue, something primitive and wonderful in their flight. They wheeled overhead, their wings beating a wild rhythm, and circled the water; then, one after another, they landed, cutting white wakes in the shining surface, calling to each other and becoming suddenly homely instead of magical as they settled for the night.

She and Dan breathed out simultaneously, and she realised that he too had been holding his breath.

'Are you going to tell me you arranged that?' he said incredulously, his voice still hushed.

'I watched, that's all. They come here every night. It's a matter of finding out when and being here at the right moment. They're quite good time-keepers, fortunately.'

His reaction pleased her. She felt that he had been as gripped as she was each time by the sense of an experience reaching way back into time. And the wings of the wild geese had borne them safely over the abrasive moment that had threatened between them.

They cycled on, comfortable with each other again, following the route Ros had worked out along quiet country lanes, until they came at last to the summit of Nab Hill, the place she had chosen for their evening picnic while they watched what she hoped would be a spectacular sunset over one of her favourite views.

'No napkins, no menu, and no choice!' she said with a touch of bravado as she took out of the saddlebag the checked gingham cloth in which she had wrapped crusty granary rolls. She had deliberately chosen the simplest of foods, but the bread was that afternoon's baking, fresh and crunchy, and the cheese came from a local farm, its flavour superb. A bottle of cider and ripe peaches, carefully wrapped in tissue paper to protect their golden bloom, joined the rolls on the cloth. 'Simple food,' Ros said. 'but I guarantee you'll enjoy it.'

'Of course I shall. You don't have to apologise for it.'

'I'm not. I'm merely pointing out that pleasures can be simple—in case you weren't aware of it.'

'You're being smug. Did I spend last Wednesday stressing how much it all cost?'

'No.'

'Well, then!' He took a roll and his white teeth bit

through its crustiness with pleasure. 'For heaven's sake, get off your hobby horse. Tell me what we can see from here.'

As they ate, Ros pointed out the landmarks on the broad floor of the valley. They talked on, forgetting time as the sky grew richer in colour, deepening fingers of gold and rose and crimson intensifying along the horizon. Light clouds had gathered, and their billowing undersides blazed with the colour of the sinking sun. The valley was flooded with vibrant gold light, the huddled villages emphasised, the river gilded, the fields lush and welcoming.

They fell silent after a while, and Dan sat watching, totally absorbed. He was leaning forward, his arms round his knees. Ros lay back, propped up on her elbows, watching his face as well as the sunset.

She remembered what he had said at Giverny about seeing the reflection of a lovely scene in someone's face, and, as she remembered, she felt the contentment in her giving way to an insidious, penetrating sadness. Something about the beauty of the moment was making her aware of how transient it all was, how far removed from reality. She didn't want this to be the last time they spent together, but she knew how useless was her yearning. She was somebody who had something Dan wanted, that was all. He knew how to be patient, to play her along like a man playing a fish on the end of a line. But once he saw that his catch was escaping him, there would be no more magic days, no more quiet, beautiful times like this. He would write her off as a bad loss and turn to fresh fields, new pursuits.

She lay back on the grass, full of an overwhelming unhappiness. She closed her eyes against the sunset. Its beauty only had the power to hurt her now as she fought against the waves of depression flooding through her, wanting to be on the way home, back to the Stables, the place that was at once her torment and her salvation.

'Ros?' She opened her eyes and he was leaning over her. 'Why are you looking like that? What is it?' Dan asked.

ecause she couldn't possibly explain her true feelings, she snatched at an inadequate substitute.

'I'm tired. I'm thinking of that long ride back.'

'No, you're not.' He was leaning closer, reading her eyes, reading her mind, and to escape him she slid away and sprang to her feet, firing a shabby taunt at him to stop his penetrating analysis.

'If you're thinking that the free entertainment extends to a romp in the grass, they you're in for a disappointment. The only physical action ahead of us is the ride home,' she said. She was instantly ashamed of her words and couldn't understand the extremes of emotion that had prompted them. Nor could she bear the way he was looking at her now as he slowly stood up.

'I don't understand you,' he said grimly. 'How can you go from watching that——' he pointed to the sunset '—and sink to the level of that scruffy gibe?'

By now she had seen the ominous black clouds rolling towards them from behind the hill.

'Just as easily as nature can swing from sunset to the storm that's racing up on us,' she said. 'Look behind you. We've no time to hang around. Unfortunately I don't have your ability to control the weather.'

'That's not the only thing you haven't got,' he said shortly. 'I doubt whether you've got a shred of normal feeling in you.'

Ros ignored his words. 'Here it comes,' she said as the first drops began to fall. She snatched up the cloth and bottle and ran over to pack them away.

Nothing was what it seemed, she thought savagely. The golden light that had bathed the valley had come from a threatening storm as much as from a beautiful sunset. This man who could look into her eyes as he had done—into her very soul, it seemed, was only concerned with her for reasons of self-interest, however much he switched on the charm.

She began to ride off down the hill, and at first when Dan called after her she ignored him, but when his voice thundered, 'Stop, can't you, you stubborn little fool!' she halted and looked back through the thickening raindrops. He was crouching down by his bike, and as she reluctantly walked back up the few yards that separated them, he said angrily, 'The chain on this tinker's contraption's broken. What do you propose to do about it?'

Ros looked helplessly at the dangling, oily links. 'Can't you mend it?'

He stood and there were white pressure-marks from his annoyance round the corners of his mouth. 'What do you think I am? A garage mechanic?'

The rain was pelting down now. Dan's hair was sleeked against his head. Her own hair was forming rats' tails and her T-shirt was clinging to her like a second skin.

' "Don't bring any money!" ' he mocked. 'What happens in your little world when something like this occurs, then? Do we wait for a miracle?'

'Don't be so obnoxious,' she said cuttingly. Then, after a moment's thought, 'I suppose you'd better phone for someone to come and get us.'

'With no money?'

'You can reverse the charges—find a house to let you call.'

'Oh, no!' he said with nasty sarcasm. 'Don't tell me you'd give in as quickly as that. You'd pretend to manage with no cash at all—but you'd be glad to rely on someone else's resources when the going gets tough. I've heard that sort of philosophy before.' He was beginning to smile now in a way she didn't like at all. 'Well—I'm sticking to our bargain. No money, no begging, and it'll take more than a few drops of rain to finish me. Just hold your horses while I think what we can do.'

Ros was furious with herself, with the wretched, treacherous weather, and most of all with him.

'If you're going to play silly devils, you can do it on your own,' she said. 'Only I don't advise sheltering under a tree. Any minute now there's going to be thunder and lightning. Enjoy your sense of virtue.'

She pushed off on her bike, determined to leave him, but she had hardly begun to pedal when she was yanked unceremoniously off the saddle and only kept from measuring her length on the streaming surface of the road by Dan's hard grip.

He let her go and turned to her bike. 'Oh, no, you don't, young lady. We're in this together, and that's the way it's going to stay.' Before her disbelieving eyes, he lifted up his foot and stamped on the chain of her own bike, and the two ends flew apart to dangle and swing uselessly. 'See how you can sail off into the sunset on that,' he said with satisfaction.

'You crazy idiot! What did you do that for?' Her voice was shrill with outrage. They stared at each other, panting, she burning with fury, he—and she could hardly believe it—actually grinning with enjoyment.

'I did it to teach you to live up to your high-flown notions instead of just paying lip-service to them,' he said smugly.

Ros looked wildly round. There was no farm, no cottage in sight, and because of the storm it was getting darker by the minute. She was beginning to shiver.

'There's a barn a bit lower down. I noticed it on the way up. I suggest we make for that,' Dan said, his tone amicable now that she was forced to share whatever mad course of action he intended initiating. 'At least it'll be dry.'

They pushed their ailing bikes downhill through the rain, Ros in sulky silence, Dan whistling something that sounded suspiciously like 'Singing in the Rain'. Ros hoped the barn would be padlocked —then let him see what he could think up to do.

But the barn was open. Bales of dusty straw left over from the previous winter were stacked at one side of its gloomy interior. At the other side were two stalls where horses must have been stabled once. There were one or two bits of mouldy tack hanging up, and blankets over the side of the stalls. Hardly a paradise, but the roof was sound.

Dan was stripping off his shirt and towelling his hair with it, showering drops of water on all sides like an enthusiastic dog. Even at the height of her annoyance, Ros could not suppress a tiny tremor of reaction to his glistening brown shoulders. Soon it would be too dark for them to see each other. Perhaps it was as well.

'I should advise you to do the same,' he said carelessly, flinging his shirt over the hay rack in the stall and picking up a blanket to shake the dust off it.

Not for anything would Ros have stood there in front of him in the scrap of a bra she wore. She wrung the edges of her T-shirt as best she could and stood there miserably rubbing the rain from her arms and legs with cold hands, then leaning forward to squeeze the wet from her hair.

Dan was maddeningly cheerful. He leapt up on top of the bales of straw and stamped to and fro. 'Not bad at all. It's years since I had a night like this. An unexpected addition to the day's treats.'

'Oh, shut up!' Ros snarled.

'No—seriously. We could do worse. The straw's got quite a bit of give in it.' He was spreading the blankets, one on top of the other, the upper one neatly turned back like a hotel bedspread.

'I don't know what you imagine that is,' Ros said ominously.

'A bed, of course. It's too dark to do anything but try to sleep while the storm blows itself out. Tomorrow at the crack of dawn I'll get you a Rolls-Royce to take you back in style. Honour will have been satisfied.'

'Pig!' She leapt up on to the straw and snatched one of the blankets. 'I'd sooner die than share these with you. I'm going to the far end. Don't come near me.'

'You'll find one blanket isn't much good. One below, one above makes more sense.' He was full of sweet reason.

Ros folded her blanket and edged between the folds. 'I presume you're getting some kind of macabre satisfaction from this situation,' she told him. 'But I'd be grateful if it could be silent satisfaction.'

He took her at her word. It was very unpleasant under the dusty blanket in wringing-wet shorts and shirt. Ros stuck it for a bit, then she stealthily wriggled out of both and spread them on the straw beside her. With every move the straw rustled.

'You haven't got fleas over there, I hope?' Dan asked through the gathering darkness, his voice mildly interested.

'Go to sleep,' she said shortly.

She lay on her back staring into the rafters, visible only when flashes of lightning briefly illuminated them. What a ridiculous situation this was, and how he would laugh about it with his friends—if he had any friends. He didn't deserve any. Heaven knew he didn't.

A soft scrabbling alerted her, somewhere to her left, where Dan was.

'What are you doing?' she asked suspiciously.

'Trying to go to sleep. What do you think?'

The rustle had stopped. Ros lay still, listening, wishing there was a lantern, a candle, anything to let her see what was going on.

The sound came again, this time the other side of her. So it wasn't him. She tensed, then made herself relax. There was bound to be a constant shifting of the straw as they breathed. She mustn't get paranoid. There it was again. The rustling went on, prolonged this time, then something brushed against her bare arm.

Ros let out a blood-curdling shriek and scrambled up. She half crawled, half staggered over the straw, the blanket caught up in her legs.

'What the hell's going on now?' he said as she crashed into him. 'This is enough to give a man a heart attack.'

'A mouse!' she gasped. 'It was creeping all round me, and then I felt it on my arm. Ooh!' She crouched against him, her teeth chattering.

He sat up, slowly so as not to knock her over. 'Well, of course there are mice. What else do you expect in a place like this? Don't tell me you're scared of them. You must have seen plenty at the Stables.'

'*Seen*, yes. Not had them creeping up on me in the dark.'

'Look—stop being silly and lie down here. At least then you'll know there's one side the wildlife's not creeping up to attack.' He was making room for her, spreading out his blanket, then taking hers and shaking it out over them both.

Ros couldn't have gone back over the bales in the dark to save her life. But how much safer was she over here? Maybe safe from mice, but what about the rat? *This* rat?

She lay rigid beside him, conscious of the warmth coming from his body, and of the bare flesh she would touch if she moved an inch. Conscious, too, of her own scanty clothing.

'I wouldn't want you to get any wrong ideas about this,' she said defiantly. 'Don't imagine there's any other reason for my being over here than to get a bit of protection from whatever's crawling around.'

'Now would I do anything so unchivalrous as misunderstand your motives?' His voice was full of innocent reproach, but he shifted slightly and she could tell that he was facing her now.

'I don't want to be here at all,' she said hurriedly.

'Of course. That's understood.'

'And just in case you get the wrong idea, let me tell you something.' She was saying too much, but she didn't seem able to stop.

'Is this absolutely necessary?' he said. 'I'd rather like to sleep if you can stifle this sudden urge for conversation.'

'It's important. When I was at college I had this craze for exotic make-up, especially frosted eyeshadow.'

'Good heavens!' he groaned. 'What's all this about?'

'Listen!' She was in a fever to convince him of her feelings, but it didn't seem to be coming out as she meant it to. 'Because I overdid the make-up, it gave people the wrong idea. Men. I spent my time convincing them that make-up was my only excess. In the end they got the message, and I got a nickname that's still applicable in one sense. The Frosted Blonde, they called me.'

He was silent, and she repeated her words.

'*Frosted*, I said. Do you hear me? And never more so than where you're concerned.'

'I hear you,' he said. With a sudden, rough movement he pulled her towards him so that his voice tickled her cheek as he went on softly. 'I hear you, Frosted Blonde. And I think you're asking to be thawed out.'

As he began to kiss her, she knew with a shock that was both exciting and humiliating that, despite her words, despite what she had told herself and told him she was feeling, she had been aching for this to happen from the start of the day. Her senses were prompting her blindly, urging her arms to creep round his neck, straining him close to her. Her body, which she had so hypocritically tried to conceal from him, was burning under his touch, and she was aware as she had never been of smooth skin and rough hair and the warmth of flesh against hers. There was no urge to resist the paths his hands and lips traced over her. The blood was singing through her veins, her whole being vibrantly alive.

Then, as suddenly as he had pulled her into his arms, he was thrusting her away from him, his hand moving up to circle her throat, holding her protesting face still.

'Not so frosty as you thought, my little puritan, are you?' he murmured, but his breathing was as disturbed as hers for a moment. His hand moved her head slightly from side to side, emphasising his words. 'Now, before we both get too involved, I suggest you go to sleep. And if you can't sleep, meditate on how many other misapprehensions you may have been labouring under in this short, misguided life of yours.'

The straw crackled noisily as he turned his back on her and shuffled himself into a comfortable position. With every bit of her still shamefully tingling with awareness, Ros lay there in the darkness, listening while his breathing steadied and slowed and deepened until she knew he was sleeping. How could he—while she was still burning with the pain of his sudden rejection of her, still speechless with the self-knowledge he had so deliberately instilled in her? Sleeping . . . after all he had done. And all he had not done, her aroused flesh cried out.

She tried to tell herself that she hated him, and at this moment she did. But hand in hand with hatred came another emotion, as far away on the scale of human feeling as anything could be, and the fusion of the two powerful forces in her felt as though it would break her.

How could she want someone who was only playing a game with her? A game in which he intended to be the winner.

CHAPTER SEVEN

ROS slept, though she had felt she never would.

Several times she shot into alert wakefulness, her heart pounding as though dreading some awful happening. But nothing happened. Only once did she imagine Dan was awake. Something about the pitch of his breathing alerted her, but she lay rigidly still, longing for daylight, and eventually slept again as she presumed he did.

When she surfaced to find sunshine flooding the barn, she turned her head cautiously to see if Dan was still there beside her.

He was sleeping, his face relaxed, those all-seeing eyes of his screened by closed lids and thick, dark lashes. With her artist's eye she looked at the planes of his face, at his mouth, sensual in the softened lines of sleep, at the dark shadows of rough beard, at the way his hair grew springing and vigorous from the side where he parted it and fell now in a way she had not seen before, in a dark wave over his forehead, so that she had an overwhelming urge to smooth it back.

What was it about one individual, one man, that against all the odds, against all the clashes of personality, against all the dictates of common sense—could render her so vulnerable? Why should his touch arouse such wildness in her? Why, when her mind knew his reasons, did her body still disregard them?

The only thing she could do was keep away from him, so that her treacherous senses didn't trap her into granting him everything he asked of her, be it the Stables or herself, because she couldn't imagine how she could hold back on anything he asked of her when that wild madness was racing through her.

Dan opened his eyes suddenly and smiled, stirring to reach out for her, but she edged out of reach, hugging the blanket to her.

'Hey!' he said softly. 'What's this? Regressing, are you?'

'No games, Dan,' she said with cold seriousness. 'This is today, remember? Yesterday's foolishness ended at midnight. Now you start behaving like a rational human being and get us out of this place.'

He pillowed his head comfortably on his arm and lay staring at her.

'Don't blame me for wanting to kiss the girl I've spent the night with "good morning". It's a natural impulse—especially when she looks as delectable as you.' Again he reached out a lazy finger, and would have run it down over the curve of her shoulder, but once more she edged away, taking the blanket with her.

'If you do that one more time you might be sorry,' he said calmly. 'The rest of my clothes are spread out to dry, and with your excessive leaning towards modesty it would be as well to leave me the blanket.'

'Oh—take it!' She flung it at him and stalked over

to retrieve her shorts and T-shirt. After all, a bikini was little more concealing than her lacy briefs and bra, and she wouldn't have cared about that. She felt the slight clamminess of her clothes with something like pleasure. She wanted to feel uncomfortable, unwashed, unfresh. Anything rather than what she had felt last night.

She could hear Dan moving, and deliberately stared out of the window of the barn. She could see along the track to where it divided lower down the hill. The sun was glinting on something, milk churns put out for collection, she thought. The trees were sparkling with raindrops still cupped in their leaves, and they sky was washed blue and fresh again.

Dan's hands suddenly touched her shoulders, and Ros jumped then tensed.

'What can you see out there?' he said in her ear.

'Nothing much,' she said, shifting slightly. 'We'd better get out and start finding civilisation. It's only a quarter to six, but someone will be stirring on a farm, and I want to be back in time to have a bath before school. I feel disgusting after those filthy blankets.'

His hands tightened on her. 'Ros——' His voice was husky, reaching some raw place deep inside her, and she steeled herself against it with difficulty.

'Don't waste your time.' She twisted out of his grip and jumped down to go over to the barn door. 'You're not going to buy me or sweet-talk me into letting you have the Stables. And you're certainly not going to get the chance to use your physical talents to further your ambitions. Cut it out, Dan.

We're both adults. We both know what your game is.'

He stood looking down at her, his face exasperated.

'Is that your considered opinion? You persist in putting the worst interpretation possible on everything I do.'

She stared back defiantly at him. 'You know it's true, so let's stop pretending.'

He leapt down and flung open the door. 'In that case, I'll go and make some arrangements with the farm. You didn't notice, by the way, but it's just round the other side of the hill. I saw it from the top.'

'Then why didn't you go there last night?' she blazed. 'There was no need at all for us to stay in this horrid place. Even if you were stupid enough to persist in making me stick the day out without spending anything, you could at least have given up after midnight.'

'I hardly think the farmer would have appreciated the niceties of our timing.' His eyes were granite-cold. 'And you forget that I had to set up my vile seduction scene. The greedy rich man and the poor innocent maiden. Well—fear no more, neither for your person nor for your property. Wait there, and a knight in shining armour will come to the rescue.'

Ros wanted to hit him to rid herself of the violence she could feel building up inside her, but he gave her one last contemptuous glance and strode off up the hill.

She hammered her fists into the doorpost, then stood sucking her knuckles, realising that there was neither sense nor joy in that.

She could hear the sound of an engine and a rattling of cans, and she saw that a milk lorry was coming along one branch of the lower track, stopping at the collection point, the driver jumping down to pick up the waiting churns.

She *would not* stay here, waiting for Dan to come back and lord it around, orchestrating their departure when and how he chose. He was out of sight over the crest of the hill now. She ran at full speed down the track to the lorry, catching it just as it started up again.

'Please——' she gasped. 'Could you give me a lift to the main road? I'd be so grateful.'

Curiosity as to what a young, rather dishevelled blonde could be doing in that isolated spot at such an unusual hour made the elderly driver tell her to hop up, and gave him the right to question her.

Ros told him half the story—the broken-down bike, being caught in a storm, the night in the barn. The half that concerned Dan she ignored.

It was sheer luck that, after another couple of pick-up points, the milkman was going to the Central Dairy, only a couple of miles from the Stables. He made a noisy, clattering detour and dropped her at the top of the drive, which went a little way towards restoring her faith in the male sex.

Ros had had her bath and got dressed, and was having coffee and toast in the kitchen before Tammy and Paul showed their sleepy faces and the inquisition began. She gave them a toned-down version and said she and Dan had spent the night at a farm, without going into details about the kind of accommodation they had had. The story sounded totally unbelievable and the whole thing quite unjustifiable.

'So what happened about the bikes?' Paul asked.

Ros's face registered guilt. She had completely forgotten them in her haste to get away from Dan.

'I'm sorry, Paul,' she confessed shamefacedly. 'Actually, I had a bit of a quarrel with Dan and hitched a lift back. I—I assume he will be seeing to the bikes.'

Paul wasn't often ruffled, but he came as close as Ros had ever seen him do to losing his temper.

'You mean you left them behind without a thought? Well, he'd just better be more responsible than you. I must say, Ros, I think you show every sign of going out of your tiny mind. How on earth two bikes break down beats me. And why you didn't phone for one of us to come and pick you up with the van I'll never understand. But somebody'll have to make good whatever damage has been done, I promise you. You'd better start praying you don't have to replace the whole bike, not a mere chain. And just don't ask to borrow anything of mine again.'

He went off upstairs in high dudgeon and Tammy pulled a sympathetic face. 'He's had that bike since his eighteenth birthday. I think it's almost got a soul in Paul's eyes.'

The phone rang and Tammy picked it up.

'Yes, she is,' she said after a pause, casting her eyes heavenwards. 'Just a moment, I'll put her on. *Dan*,' she mouthed as she handed over the receiver.

Ros took it, feeling less than eager to speak to him.

'Yes?'

'I suppose you think that was clever?' he said coldly. 'The fact that you're at the end of the phone is, I suppose, one degree better than my not having a clue where you are, but I must say thankfulness is not my strongest emotion at this very moment.'

'Then why bother to phone?'

'Because a) I wanted to know that you hadn't been picked up by some psychopath. Have you never been warned against hitching lifts? Goodness knows, the police have had enough to say about it. And b) there happens to be the little matter of two bikes which you so blithely forgot.'

'I presume you've dealt with them?' she said, unmoved. 'The whole affair was largely your responsibility, after all.'

'You presume too damned much! But yes, I am dealing with them. They will be repaired and delivered to the Stables later this afternoon. In the meantime you will apologise to Paul for any inconvenience caused and tell him that the damage will be made good at my expense.'

'*I* shall pay for the repair of the damage to Paul's bike, which was quite accidental,' Ros told him with determination. 'You can certainly pay for what you did to mine, since it was entirely your fault.'

Tammy's eyes widened as she listened unashamedly.

'Oh—don't be so childish!' He spoke through a yawn. 'I've had enough of this nonsense. Just one more thing. I shall be staying at the Dower House this weekend. I warn you because I assume that, like myself, you would prefer we didn't meet.'

'Don't worry. You'll be left in complete isolation.'

'Not complete,' he said. 'Karen will be there to give me her view of the house. I fancy she'll be rather easier to get along with than you are.'

'Easier in every way. And I don't suppose you'll be the first to find that out!' Ros said nastily, and slammed the phone down.

'Gosh, Ros! I honestly think you're undergoing a personality change,' Tammy said. 'I haven't heard you be so rude to anyone as you are to him.'

'You haven't heard the half of it!' Ros said bitterly. 'And I certainly haven't got either the time or the inclination to tell you now. I'm going to be late. Is it all right if I take the van? Or do you want to take me in and bring me back?'

'You can take it. I'm in today, and Paul said he was too. But you can't run away from things forever!' Tammy called after her as she ran out of the house.

Why was Dan moving into the Dower House? Ros asked herself as she drove along. Was it to make her realise how uncomfortable it would be for her if he were around permanently at the big house while she persisted in hanging on to the Stables?

She sighed heavily. While they were involved in angry argument, she could lose herself in the fight. But, when she thought about the situation from this distance, she just felt wretched. And it wasn't just a question of his making life difficult for her if he didn't get his own way. It was a matter of whether she could bear to go on seeing him around. Where was the sense in setting up such a situation of self-torture? Look how she'd reacted when he mentioned Karen. That was only talking about it. How would she behave when it came to seeing the two of them together?

Maybe she would be able to cope if she brought someone else into her own life. There was Alan's suggestion of closer friendship waiting to be taken up. It wouldn't be a case of deceiving him. He knew exactly how she felt, and if he could take the risk, then why shouldn't she be willing, too?

And work. She must fling herself into her work. Give herself no time to think non-stop about Dan as she seemed to have been doing. Mental discipline, that was what she needed.

That morning she got the children to paint an emotion, and as an example she dashed off an illustration of anger—an explosive burst of violent whorls of red and purple spiked with jabs of black. It made her feel considerably better, and proved that her art therapy was valid.

At lunch time she went in to see Alan, primarily to ask if she could take Debra out to the Cotswold Farm Park for the promised visit on the coming Sunday.

'It's a quiet weekend for me, so this would be a good time,' she told him.

He checked his desk diary. 'Fine. There's nothing special on at school this weekend, and Debra seems well at the moment. She'll enjoy it.'

'Good. I'll pick her up about eleven so that she can have lunch at our place, then we can get an early start. And I'd better have one of the lightweight folding chairs, if that's all right. It'll be rough ground and not really suitable for her own electric one.'

'I'll fix that. I'm sorry I can't offer to come and give you a hand, but I'm committed to going over to see my father this Sunday.' Alan paused, looking diffidently at her. 'You mentioned a quiet weekend. Does that mean you're not doing anything Saturday night?'

'Nothing at all.'

'Then what about coming to the Town Hall? It's a Beethoven night. I'm sure I can get you a ticket and wangle two together somewhere. Would you like that?'

'Yes, I would. That would be lovely.' She smiled determinedly, hoping the result looked genuine.

'You look a bit tired today. Anything bothering you?'

'Plenty, but nothing you can help me with. It's nothing to do with Gateway.'

'You're sure there isn't anything else you'd rather be doing on Saturday night? No—no one with a prior claim?'

'No one at all.' Ros wished Alan wouldn't be so diffident. Didn't that illustrate her own contrariness, though? One man too forceful in his pursuit of what he wanted, one man not forceful enough.

'Actually,' he said, 'the Carters are going too and they invited me back for supper afterwards. They'll be glad for you to go along as well, I know.'

Ros felt trapped. A cosy foursome. But it was her

own fault, and now she would have to go through with it.

She went to find Debra and tell her about Sunday, and was further thrown when the little girl's first question was whether Dan would be coming with them.

'I'm afraid you'll have to make do with me,' Ros told her. 'Dan's a very busy man, you know.'

'He came in to see us last Sunday.' Debra was quite unaware of how much she was surprising her listener. 'He stayed to tea and he talked to Alan quite a lot.'

'Well, wasn't that nice of him?' Ros wondered what the reason was for both visit and talk. He hadn't said a word to her about it. Nor had Alan. That in itself was suspicious.

'So he's not all that busy,' Debra went on.

'He's busy this weekend. He's got a guest—a lady guest.'

Debra's head tilted to one side as she surveyed Ros knowingly.

'You're jealous, aren't you? I knew you were a bit cross today.'

'I'm nothing of the kind,' Ros said firmly. 'And you are full of far too many ideas about grown-up matters, young lady. Shouldn't you be at physiotherapy? Off you go!'

Debra giggled and went obediently on her way. Impudent she might be, but at least she was thinking of things other than her own problems, Ros thought as she watched her go.

But Dan . . . What was in his devious mind? Or

was he genuinely, disinterestedly concerned for once? She doubted it.

The bikes had been returned and were leaning against the wall of the house when she got home. Ros phoned the nearest cycle repair shop and got a rough estimate of the cost of a chain repair. She wrote a cheque, put it in an envelope marked 'Paul's bike', and, after making sure that Dan's car was nowhere around, she slipped it through the letterbox of the Dower House. That was one minor matter settled between them.

Or not settled, as she discovered later in the week when she picked up the morning post and found an unstamped envelope addressed to herself among it.

When she opened it and pulled out the folded sheet of paper it contained, a shower of torn up scraps fell on the floor—the remains of her cheque. On the sheet of paper Dan had written three words only. 'Don't be childish'.

She refrained from a repetition of the farce. She had tried to pay her share, and she supposed he would hardly miss a bill a hundred times greater than the one he had paid.

Ros worked hard all day Friday on an order, and filled Saturday morning and afternoon with work on a watercolour. Since she had no wish to go anywhere near the Dower House and the path skirted it far too closely, Daks had to do without his usual walks on that day.

By the end of Saturday afternoon, though, his canine cunning discovered the window Paul had left open in the larder, and he escaped to do his own walking. Ros was compelled to go after him, and it was with a sinking heart that she heard barking coming from the Dower House lawn.

Forced into it, she pushed through the gap in the fence and saw Karen backed up against the summer-house, a garden chair overturned on the lawn. She was flapping a gauzy scarf at Daks, who thought the whole thing was an uproarious game and was alternately crouching and wagging his tail, and then darting towards the terrified Karen.

'Shoo! Shoo! Go away, you nasty brute!' she was saying ineffectually.

'Daks!' At Ros's firm voice, the dog turned and raced towards her and she grabbed his collar and hung on to him. 'I'm sorry. He got out,' she told Karen. 'He's really only playing. We have an old scarf that he has tugs of war with. I expect he thought you were going to do the same.'

Karen righted the chair and collapsed into it, fanning herself with the scarf. 'He certainly fooled me. I've never liked dogs. Such excitable, pushy creatures. I've forgotten your name—but you're the little girl who came in with Dan the other night, aren't you?'

'Yes, and the name's Ros.' *Cow*, Ros thought. But Karen seemed quite unaware of the patronising tone of her words.

'Come and talk to me if that brute will let you,' the girl went on. 'Have a glass of this. It started out as Bucks Fizz, but there's not a lot of fizz left in it, I'm afraid.' She poured some out and handed a crystal glass to Ros. 'I made it after lunch and Dan was supposed to be coming out, but he's been fiddling around with plans for this place all day. He's been a lousy host. I'm bored to tears.'

Ros felt a sneaking satisfaction as she murmured her sympathy, but it was short-lived.

'At least I've persuaded him to take me dancing tonight, though,' Karen went on. 'There's nothing much to do round here, is there? I couldn't bear living with all this nature around. Give me a city penthouse any day.'

'I'm very fond of this place,' Ros said stiffly.

'I suppose it's a matter of what you're used to. I wasn't cut out to be a peasant.'

'I don't suppose you were.' Ros looked at the smart, unsuitable dress—the last thing to wear for lounging around in a country garden. Karen's fingers on the glass were perfectly manicured. She didn't look as though she would get any pleasure from pulling up the weeds that were crying out to be dealt with, and the high heels of her sling-back sandals must have sunk into the grass with every step she took across the lawn.

'Oh, well—I hope you enjoy tonight, anyway,' she said insincerely, and took her leave, thankful that at least she hadn't bumped into Dan.

Her own Saturday night was a fairly depressing business. She found her mind straying far too often, while the orchestra played, to Dan and the problems he had created in her life. Thoughts of the kind of music and dancing that were featuring in his own Saturday night were not comfortable. That was the trouble with music. It allowed your subconscious too much room to make itself felt. At the moment that was the last thing she wanted.

Supper with the Carters had a boring, middle-class cosiness about it. They were welcoming, and she felt very guilty about not enjoying herself more, but she hated being made to feel part of a foursome. It shaped her, pinned her down at Alan's side in a way that just didn't feel right. It had been a big mistake, she decided miserably as Alan drove her home.

'I won't ask you in, if you don't mind, Alan,' she said as they turned into the Stables yard. 'I'm really tired tonight.'

'That's all right. It was a lovely evening, wasn't it? Let's do it again.' His affectionate, totally unaccusing goodnight kiss saved her the necessity of answering.

'I don't expect I'll see you tomorrow,' Ros told him. 'But I'll make sure Debra's back before bedtime.'

You can't do it, she thought unhappily as she went upstairs. You just can't make do with anyone, not even someone as nice as Alan. Emotions wouldn't be appeased in that facile way.

How was Dan's evening? she wondered with a stab of jealousy. Was Karen the kind of company he really liked? She was attractive enough. Harmless, in her own way. Certainly talented musically. But would she look twice at water-lilies growing on a lake, or geese circling to land on the shining surface of an upland reservoir?

Stop it! she told herself. It's nothing to do with

you. And Dan only pretended to appreciate the things that appeal to you, so who are you kidding.

The owner of the gallery where Paul exhibited had taken him and Tammy into town to an exhibition of watercolours at the City Art Gallery on Sunday, so Ros and Debra were alone for lunch. Ros cooked Debra's favourite meal, chicken and peas and jacket potatoes, and made a kiwi-fruit cheesecake which Debra pronounced the best she had tasted.

'Now, we won't hang around doing dishes,' Ros said when they had eaten, piling everything into the sink. 'We want as long as possible at the Farm Park.'

There was a knock on the door as she was speaking.

'And I'll soon get rid of whoever that is,' she promised, thinking that one of their friends had dropped in uninvited, as often happened at the weekend.

It was a bolt from the blue to find Dan leaning against the wall when she opened the door.

'What is it you do to me?' he said without preamble. 'I find you totally exasperating when I'm with you, and irritatingly unforgettable when I'm not. You spoil my sleep by crashing in on my dreams, and when I'm awake I seem to be more and more in two minds—one fuming about you, and one struggling with what I'm supposed to be doing. You've ruined my weekend. I found Karen, poor girl, as boring as can be.'

Ros found a voice at last. 'Don't be so rude about

the girl. And don't talk such a lot of nonsense.'

'It isn't nonsense. You are without a shadow of doubt the most obtrusive personality I have ever encountered.'

'So don't go out of your way to encounter me. I'm not asking you to. The reverse, in fact. And the only reason you keep thinking about me is that you haven't got your own way. It's known as a temper tantrum among mothers of toddlers.'

'A tongue like acid, and still I listen,' he said, shaking his head. 'I've decided that all I can do is come over and take you out somewhere. What's the point of not seeing you if you're still in my mind? Do you know Karen went off in a huff this morning? Even she noticed that I'm somewhat preoccupied. So come on, Ros. Get your knuckledusters on and come out with me.'

Ros hardened her resolve in the face of the barrage of charm she was being subjected to. 'So sorry I can't fall in with this latest whim at the drop of a hat, but I have a guest. I'm taking Debra out.'

'Then I'll take the two of you.'

She began to close the door. 'You'll do no such thing. How can you have the barefaced cheek to come round here without a trace of an apology for Monday?'

'What is there to apologise for? For making you stick to your principles? I was doing you a favour. Do I ask you to apologise for your disappearing act? Come on, Ros?'

'Go away. You're not coming,' Ros hissed. The scene was becoming ludicrous, with both of them hanging on to the door and arguing in low voices so that Debra wouldn't hear.

'We'll see about that!' He wrenched the door from her grip and leapt past her through the lobby, slowing down to a relaxed stroll as he entered the kitchen.

'Hi, Debra. How would you like a male chauffeur for your trip? Here I am on offer.'

The little girl's face had lit up at the sight of him. 'Dan! Great! I wanted you to come. I told Ros so.'

'Did you? And she thought I couldn't make it?' He flashed a knowing look at Ros. 'Well, I can, so you've got your wish. Shall we go, girls?' He beamed maddeningly at both of them.

Ros couldn't show her feelings in front of Debra, but her eyes flashed fire in his direction. 'Could you just come outside a moment, Dan?' she asked sweetly. 'I'll give you something to put in the car before we all go out.'

She closed the kitchen door and the house door behind them, then rounded on him.

'Of all the despicable, dirty tricks!'

'Yes, wasn't it? But rather smart, and there isn't a thing you can do about it. I know you wouldn't dream of upsetting Debra and spoiling her day.'

'You louse!' Ros said with feeling.

'True. Tell me later, when we're alone. Right now, let's give the kid a good day out, shall we?'

As he so infuriatingly had pointed out, there wasn't a thing she could do about it. Fortunately Debra was so effervescent with excitement at having Dan there and so intrigued at riding in his car that she noticed nothing. Ros insisted that the little girl had the front seat, saying that it was her day out and of course she must sit by Dan. Sitting in the back, she was covered as far as any tendency to silence on her own part was concerned.

Once they reached the Farm Park, it was really impossible to hang on to any vestige of anger. Set on a high slope of the wold, the farm bred rare breeds of cattle and other domestic animals, and who could do other than laugh at their gentle inquisitiveness and friendly behaviour?

Dan carried Debra piggy-back for a great deal of the time, and crouched to sit her on his knee in the pen where children could wander freely among the Indian goats and rabbits and Runner ducks, so for once she was free of her chair. She laughed until she cried when one of the goats insisted on licking her bare leg.

'Take it away! It tickles!' she said, convulsed with delight.

'Ros?' Dan said, looking at her. 'Not scared of these, too, are you?'

'No. Not at all,' Ros said, hurriedly rearranging her features which had, she realised, been frozen in sudden shock.

'You just looked a bit off for a moment,' he went on, raising his eyebrows in question. Ros caught his eye and shook her head imperceptibly, turning to Debra.

'See those hens with feathered feet, Debs? They look as though they're wearing trousers.'

The delights of the park occupied them again and

were endless. There were longhorn cattle, huge-eyed and docile in spite of their horns. A litter of Oxfordshire pigs, half grown, lay side by side as neatly as sardines in a tin. Highland cattle peered, bright-eyed, through their sandy-coloured shaggy coats. But the star item, they all agreed, was a litter of ten black and white piglets, unbelievably tiny, who would suddenly take it into their heads to career around the field as though a gale blew them through the grass, squealing loudly and sending Debra into paroxysms of laughter again.

When they eventually left—not before closing time—they sang all the way back to Gateway. Ros could hardly believe that she had set off in such a bad temper. When Dan chose to be charming, there was no resisting him. But something else had lifted the day into the category of very special, something she was nursing impatiently inside herself, a secret bursting to be told.

Debra gave them both bone-crushing hugs, and they left her in the lounge giving a vivid account of her day to her friends. Ros asked Dan to wait for her while she went in to see the Matron.

When she came out and sat in the seat beside him in the car he turned to her at once.

'Come on. Tell me. You've been fizzing over something half the day. What was it you saw Matron about?'

'Did it show so much?'

'Only to me. I'm particularly attuned to your moods, remember.'

Ros rested her head back on the leather seat and

looked at him.

'It was the goat. Remember what Debra said when we were in the pets' enclosure and you had her on your knee?'

'You mean when she told it to go away?'

'Because it was *tickling* her. Dan—she hasn't been able to feel anything at all in her legs since the accident. Today she did, without realising it.'

'For heaven's sake!' he exploded. 'Why didn't you tell her? Are you saying there's hope she'll walk again?'

'I think it could be possible. But I'm not qualified to know for certain. It's the mind I deal with, remember. Not the body. Someone else who understands the full extent of the damage she suffered has to handle that. Suppose I raise her hopes for nothing?'

Dan thumped the wheel in frustration. 'So we wait and see. For how long?'

'Matron's going to speak to the doctor tomorrow.'

'Why not tonight? Why not at once?'

'Dan——' Ros put out a hand and touched his arm. 'Even if I'm right and the signs are good, it's going to be a slow business. It will take months of physiotherapy and patient exercise. Nothing will work an overnight miracle.'

He started up the engine. 'I tell you something; that job I could not do—haven't got the patience. But I certainly admire those of you who stick in there and do it. And I know why you get so attached to the place.'

They drove back to the Stables, thoughts of Debra

and hopes for her strong in both their minds.

'Your friends are home, I see,' Dan said, looking at the lights in the Stables. He switched off the engine outside the courtyard entrance. 'Well, not such a bad afternoon after all, was it?'

All animosity had been driven out of Ros.

'Not bad at all,' she said, giving him a slow smile.

'And now it's time to say goodnight.' His eyes holding hers, he leaned towards her.

'Dan——' She attempted to push him away.

'Look—I kissed Debra goodnight. I kissed all her friends goodnight, even. I kiss all the girls. What's so special about you?' His arms pulled her towards him, crushing her feeble opposition.

The thing that was special about her was that, when Dan kissed her, it could never be casual. She resisted him because she knew that, the instant his lips touched hers, she would respond like a flower opening to the sun, as she was doing now. Somehow her arms were round his neck, straining him to her, and she was betrayed once more by her own senses.

'Dan!' Ros made a mammoth effort and pulled away from him. 'This is no good!'

His voice was full of amusement. 'I thought it was very good indeed.'

'Don't joke!' She scrambled out of the car and turned to face him. 'We have to settle this business. You can't go on with this perpetual hope that I'm going to let you have the Stables. I'm not, Dan. I'm going to stay here. Karen told me you'd been working on the plans. You *must* count this place out.'

He stretched, deliberately casual. 'I don't think you need worry. I have a compromise in mind that may satisfy both of us. You see, I think I know you better than you know yourself, Ros. I think there's something you want more than your precious bit of property.'

'Dan, listen to me!'

'I have. I've listened to what you've said and to what you haven't said. Now you're going to have to wait just a little longer, and everything will work out. Goodnight, Ros.'

He smiled calmly at her and drove off towards the Dower House.

Ros watched the car disappear. She felt helpless, like Canute defying the ocean, like an idiot forbidding the sun to rise. Whatever she did, whatever she said, Dan went implacably on, sure that in the end he would get his own way—or something so near to it that it would satisfy him.

Suddenly exhausted, wanting home, she turned and went towards the lights of the Stables.

CHAPTER EIGHT

THREE days passed, and Dan seemed to have disappeared off the face of the earth again.

The calm had the quality of a lull in a siege for Ros. It was ominous rather than restful. How soon would she be told what Dan had in mind now? It was all very well for him to talk of compromise, but what compromise could there possibly be when two people wanted entirely different courses of action? The thing that truly frustrated her more than anything was her own powerlessness. Heaven knew she had tried, but nothing seemed to make Dan accept that she meant what she said. Each time she attempted to convince him, all she succeeded in doing was sparking off some new strategy to win her over to his way of thinking.

The one glowing, bright spot was the news she was given on Tuesday that the doctors consulted thought there was a strong chance of Debra's regaining at least a measure of mobility. Ros felt like crying when she saw the transformation in the child's eyes. It was as though a light had been switched on that she hadn't known was there. The good news sent a wave of restlessness flooding through the school, something that inevitably happened when the children's hard-won acceptance of disability was broken by sudden hope for one of them, so there was little time for Ros to brood over her own problems, on work days at least.

Debra's reprieve put things in a certain perspective. Wrangling over property seemed so unworthy in comparison—if wrangling over property was really what she and Dan were engaged in. Sometimes the question of the Stables seemed like the tip of a dark iceberg, the bulk of what was really the issue between them hidden below the surface.

At the end of Thursday afternoon, when Ros was about to leave the school, Alan called her into his office. There was an air of suppressed excitement about him as he closed the door.

'I thought you hadn't an earthly chance of succeeding when you first broached the subject, Ros,' he enthused. Ros hadn't the remotest idea what he was talking about. 'You pulled it off, though! You really did. Miracle worker!'

Normally so calm and controlled, he seized her in a bear-hug and spun her round.

'Alan! What on earth are you talking about?' she gasped breathlessly as she extricated herself. 'What miracle? If you mean Debra, I can't claim credit for that. Somebody would have noticed something sooner or later.'

'Not just Debra! Debra and all the rest. The whole school—that's what I mean!' He suddenly seemed to realise what a very uncharacteristic turn his behaviour had taken, and straightened his tie with a sheepish grin. 'Sorry, Ros. I was just so damned pleased. And it's only just happened.'

'Then maybe you ought to tell me *what*—and I'll join in too.'

'You mean he really hasn't said anything at all to you?'

'Who, Alan? Begin at the beginning.'

He looked at her incredulously. 'Dan Maxton. I really thought you were in on all this.'

Ros swallowed. 'I know nothing. Tell me.' Dan's name had aroused a feeling of foreboding in her, and she sat down on a chair while Alan perched on the edge of his desk.

'Maxton's just been on the phone. He's decided to put money into Gateway—a lot. Enough to keep us going for the foreseeable future. The pressure's off, Ros. Isn't it fantastic news?'

Something held Ros back from sharing Alan's delight. She knew she ought to be as up in the air as he was, but it took a conscious effort for her to say, 'That's wonderful, Alan. Really great.'

The trouble was that at the back of her mind she couldn't silence the big question, why? Why, after his adamant squashing of her own first raising of the idea of his possibly helping the school, had Dan turned round so completely now?

'And does the school stay here?' she asked.

'Yes. He said he'd noticed several areas where improvement could be made. Haven't we all? But he thought the basic premises were sound and well-designed.'

So there was no question of a change of opinion about the use to which the Dower House was to be put. Ros had known that, really. It would have been foolish to imagine that there might be. Where would the compromise be in that? It would be total capitulation, and Dan was the last man on earth to take that course.

'So what exactly did he say?' she persisted.

'A lot of nice things about Gateway, first of all. Then he told me what he was thinking of doing, and said that the way was clear from his point of view, but we would have to approach the Council carefully. He's right about that. There'll be all their legal bods looking for flaws and creating mounds of paperwork—but they wouldn't turn down an offer like this. I know they had other ideas for the land we're on, but think of the adverse publicity if the press got wind of any rejection of support for Gateway.'

'And he gave no reason for his sudden decision? I told you that he was hardly enthusiastic in response to my tentative suggestions.'

'He just said he'd come round to thinking that we were well worth saving—or there was a lot of point in saving us. Something along those lines. I forget his exact words. He was impressed by the work we were doing, et cetera. Does it really matter? I honestly think if we got to the bottom of it, it would be young Debra we had to thank. He's got a soft spot for that kid. He didn't say so in so many words—probably thought it bad form to pick out one child from so many as having enlisted his sympathy and practical support. But he did say something about a certain young lady's pleasure in the school's continuing to function being his reward, he hoped. I took that to mean Debra.'

Ros stored the words away for future consideration, uneasily aware that to her mind at least they could be ambiguous. However, it was unfair to Alan to spoil his moment of relief and jubilation by dwelling on what significance they could have for herself.

'I'm delighted, Alan, really!' she told him as she stood. 'I should have been unbelievably sad to see the end of Gateway.'

'I certainly feel that a load has been lifted from my mind.' He looked directly at her. 'It doesn't change anything between us, Ros. I wasn't panicked into saying what I did about the way I feel about you. I meant it. And I'm doubly grateful to Dan Maxton for ensuring that there's no immediate danger of your being forced to look for employment somewhere else miles away from me.'

His sincerity, and the burden it placed on her, was too much. Ros surprised herself and him by suddenly bursting into tears.

'I'm sorry,' she gulped, while Alan stood looking helplessly at her.

'No, Ros. *I'm* sorry. It was inconsiderate of me. I know you haven't got cause to be quite so pleased with Dan Maxton from your own personal viewpoint. I get so involved with school that I forget you have problems of your own. What's happening about the Stables?'

'I don't know what's happening about anything—and I don't even feel sure I know what I

want to happen any more.' Her sudden outburst
was over, and Ros was angry with herself for her
display of weakness. She pushed her hair back
impatiently and stuffed her handkerchief back in her
pocket. 'Oh—I'm going, Alan. I don't want to talk
about it, and I certainly don't feel justified in
depressing you when something to be thankful for
has happened for once.'

She turned the implication of Dan's intervention
in the Gateway issue over and over in her mind as
she cycled home. It certainly changed things as far as
she was concerned. With him involved in her
working environment, as well as developing yet
another branch of his many businesses on her
doorstep, what hope of a peaceful existence was
there?

Maybe that was his intention. Could he be so
diabolically persistent as to be deliberately hounding
her on all sides, even killing her with kindness by
saving her school, so that she was both pushed and
shamed into letting him buy her out of the Stables?
Or was she just being over-fanciful, seeing threat
where no threat was intended?

She completed the journey on automatic pilot,
and it wasn't until she turned into the drive that she
came back to earth.

There was noise. She could hear it from the end of
the drive nearest the main road. Voices, machinery,
the clanging of metal and the clattering of timber on
timber.

This morning, when she had instinctively glanced
in spite of herself to see if Dan's car was there in

front of the Dower House, all had been quiet. Now,
as she drew nearer, she could see that the place was a
hive of industry. There was a huge lorry from which
building supplies were being unloaded. Scaffolding
had been erected the whole width of the frontage of
the house, and men were up there, scrambling over
the roof, doing something to the gutters.

The speed of it all sickened her. Was Dan already
so confident that he was going to win the day? Even
before he had spoken to her?

She got off her bike and leaned it against the
gatepost, then went over to the man who looked to
be in charge, and who was checking off items as they
were unloaded from the lorry.

'Is Mr Maxton here?' she asked.

'No. Haven't seen him since this morning when
we started. He should be coming back before
knocking-off time, though. Anything I can do?' He
seemed a decent enough man—no ogre, even if he
was engaged in ogre's work in Ros's eyes.

'No, thanks. I need to speak to Mr Maxton
personally.' She looked round. 'All this is very
sudden, isn't it?'

The man grinned. 'You get used to that in this
job. Mr Maxton tends to want things done yesterday
once he gets an idea. He phoned in and pulled us off
another job first thing today. "Right, Bannister,"
he told me. "Things seem to be sorting themselves
out on the Dower House job now. I want it given top
priority." So that was it. Here we are and here we
stay till the job's done—and if the other lot who've
been left in the lurch complain, that's their tough

luck. Are you the young lady at the other place over there through the trees?' He nodded towards the Stables.

'One of them, yes.'

'In that case, we might have to inconvenience you a bit sometimes. We'll need to turn the water off, and the power, for some of the time, and apparently your supply leads off this one. We'll give you notice, of course. Mr Maxton said to mention it.'

Was that another second-hand threat that life could become very difficult?

'Tell him I'd like to see him when he comes, would you?' Ros said. She walked over in the direction of the gap in the fence, but when she reached the end of the house, the point where she could see the old summer-house, she stopped dead in her tracks, devastated by the sight that confronted her.

The thatched roof of the summer-house was gone, torn off and reduced to a heap of rubbish, piled up on a patch of bare earth. A workman was stooping over it, putting a match to the newspaper stuffed under it. Thick plastic sheeting was stretched over the shell of the building Max had so loved, and timber was stacked inside. The chairs were nowhere to be seen.

Somehow this brought home the pain of the whole business more than anything else had done. It was as though Dan had deliberately given the destruction of the summer-house top priority to make his point that the old times were over. This was his territory, and he could do what he liked with it. If he chose to fill the Dower House with strangers, people there for a good time and a well-cooked meal, people who had never known Max, then he had every right to do so. It was nothing to do with her.

But it didn't make her feel any less bad about it.

'All right, love?' The workman looked up at her, standing back as the flames caught and the dry straw began to crackle and blaze.

Ros pulled herself together. 'Just taken aback. I was fond of that old summer-house. There was someone who used to sit there watching the birds . . .'

'Seen a good bit of life, this place, I should imagine,' the man said. He forked the straw into the centre of the blaze. 'Let the wet in, this old stuff did. You could see daylight through it. Gone for birds' nests, I shouldn't wonder. That lot's solid oak in there.' he pointed to the timber stacked under the plastic in the shell of the summer-house. 'Mr Maxton wanted it kept dry until he could get it in the house, and we can't do that until the furniture's gone.'

The chain of events stretched inexorably forward. Today the summer-house. Tomorrow, or some time soon, the furniture. Then the shape of the house would change, the garden would be altered, the trees—some of them—would be cut down to make room for the car park.

'You're sure you're all right?' the man repeated. 'Been hot today, hasn't it?'

It wasn't the man's fault. 'I just don't care for changes,' Ros told him.

'You wouldn't do for our job, then. We spend our

lives taking things apart and putting them together again one way or another. We do a good job, though—and that's a promise.'

Ros smiled tiredly. 'I'm sure you do.'

She went on through the gap in the fence and along to collect her bike at the courtyard entrance.

Tammy and Paul were still working—or at least Paul was, and Tammy was in there talking to him. Ros could hear the tap of his hammer on the chisel and the low murmur of their voices. She went past quietly, not wanting to speak to anyone else just now. A ball of anger and pain had built up inside her.

In the kitchen she could still hear the noise from the Dower House. Daks was padding to and fro, whining restlessly, disturbed by the unfamiliar activity. The clattering and the shouting voices smothered the gentle woodland sounds they were attuned to, and it was as though there was no wind in the leaves, no bird call from tree to tree. She imagined the range of sounds that would replace the present clamour. Car engines revving up. Music maybe, on still nights. People talking as they came and went. Nothing would be the same.

She went upstairs and filled the bath, wanting something to melt away the ache building up inside her, but as she lay in the scented water there was no easing of her unhappiness. On the contrary, it was becoming painfully clear that what hurt her so very much was that it was Dan doing all these things, Dan who didn't care about her feelings, only about what he wanted to do.

If she hated him, it would be easier to cope with the whole situation, but he had been too clever to let that happen. He had charmed his way under her defences and into her heart, and she didn't hate him. Not at all. What she couldn't bear was that the man who had been so kind to Debra, who had appeared to show such sensitivity in so many ways, could be so ruthlessly uncaring in others. How could he have bought his way into her working life as he had done? Oh, he was saving the school, she knew that. But at the same time he was destroying her. Today, for the first time, she didn't know whether she was tough enough to go on fighting him.

From the bedroom window, as she changed into jeans and a shirt, she could see the roof of the Dower House. She imagined the two new wings extending behind it, and turned away from the window to brush her hair savagely, wishing she could brush the thoughts out of her head as easily as she could remove the tangles from her hair.

Paul and Tammy had come into the kitchen, and Tammy was standing peeling potatoes at the sink. She dropped the potato into the bowl as Ros entered, and went over to stand at Paul's side.

'You've seen them?' she asked Ros.

Ros nodded. 'Pretty depressing, isn't it?'

'Ros,' Paul said, 'we've got to talk to you.'

Ros looked from one to the other of them, then pulled out a chair. 'I don't know what else can happen today,' she said wearily, 'but you look as though something's about to. Go ahead. Talk.'

'Well, it isn't all bad,' Tammy hurried to say.

'Some of it's very good, in fact. I'm sure you'll think so.'

'We were hoping you'd have got your affairs sorted out, but we're not sure just where you are in that respect, and things are getting a bit urgent as far as we're concerned,' Paul said. 'I'll start at the beginning with me. You know I've been doing more and more work for the Ikon lately? Well, Graham Winterton has been hinting for some time that he'd like me to be more closely involved in the running of the place. I took it with a pinch of salt at first. You know how people talk. But he's come up with a definite offer now. He's intending to open a new place in London, and he wants to be able to concentrate all his own efforts on that side of things. So he's offered me the job of running the Ikon—selecting work for display, making new contacts, organising special shows. That sort of thing. A bit of an unexpected challenge as far as I'm concerned, but I'm keen to have a go at it.'

'I should think so!' Ros exclaimed, but Paul held up a hand to stop her.

'The thing is, it means moving over there. There's a big flat that runs over the gallery and the dress shop next door. And there's plenty of room for my own work out at the back. Graham owns a row of garages, and I can spread out into a couple of those with my machinery. So that's that part of it. It's ideal, really, but for the fact that it sorts of breaks things up here.'

Ros went over to hug him. 'It's wonderful news, Paul. Don't regret it for one minute. It's a great opportunity for you, and of course you're going to take it.' She stood back, looking at both of them and seeing the proud way Tammy was looking at Paul and the way her hand had slipped into his. 'But you come into this somewhere, don't you, Tammy? Let's have the rest of it.'

'Well——' Tammy blushed and looked at Paul. 'Shall I tell her?'

'Go ahead. I've had my say.'

'Well—we've talked about all this a lot over the past couple of weeks. Paul just had to talk to someone. He was worried about leaving here while all this business over you and the Stables was going on. And the more we talked about it, the more we began to realise that as well as everything else, we were both not very happy about being separated.'

'So the long and short of it is that I've asked Tammy to come with me. It's a big enough flat for a married couple. Having regular money means we can afford it. And she seems to think it's a good idea.' Paul attempted to look blasé and completely failed.

'So it's both of us, Ros,' Tammy said, her eyes pleading. 'We're sorry it's happened right now, but Graham's pushing for a decision or he'll have to approach someone else to run the Ikon.'

Ros knew that she couldn't let them suspect that she felt as though the bottom was dropping out of her world.

'Stop apologising for the fact that my two favourite people have the good sense to hang on to each other,' she said, kissing them both. 'I suppose

I've always taken it for granted that you two would get together eventually. The last couple of weeks I've been too wrapped up in my own affairs to see the pace quickening.'

'We know, and we'd feel a lot happier if you'd already chosen to go somewhere new yourself rather than us moving out and leaving you behind here under the present circumstances,' Paul said.

'This isn't the time to talk about me,' Ros said firmly, getting up and taking three glasses from the cupboard. 'Get a bottle out, Paul, and let's have a drink to celebrate something good, for heaven's sake.'

She managed to keep up her act well enough while they talked and drank their way through a bottle of Lambrusco, but when Tammy invited her to come over and see the flat at the Ikon and then go out for a Chinese meal, Ros asked to be given a rain-check.

'I'd love to see the flat, but not tonight, if you don't mind. There's something I've got to do, and if I put if off until later I shan't get round to it.' She began clearing away the glasses. 'Leave these. I'll see to them. Go and enjoy a meal by yourselves and I'll celebrate with you later.'

Ros felt she couldn't have kept on smiling a minute longer. The instant the door closed behind them and they drove off in the little van, she sank into a chair, dejection flooding into every vein.

Daks came over and rested his head on her lap. She looked down at him, stroking his head until her hand suddenly froze.

'Oh, Daks! How on earth do we divide you

between us?' she said. She slipped down beside him and buried her face in his warm, doggy-smelling fur, crying and having her tears licked away by his rough tongue.

But the tears were a self-indulgence she couldn't allow herself for long, and in any case, crying over Daks was ridiculous. He had always been her dog by his own choice, and Paul and Tammy had each other. They weren't going to fight her for the dog.

What she had to do now was try to think sanely and sensibly about her own options. Her world had fallen apart around her many times before. For a time here at the Stables she had believed that she had found security that would last, security in a place of her own. But where was that security now? Somehow the place seemed to be losing its importance. Tammy and Paul were leaving. She was going to be alone here, just her and Daks, with the sounds of other people's lives coming to taunt her from the Dower House. There would be hostile and inevitable encounters both on home ground and at school with a man who was accustomed to getting what he wanted, and in whose way she had thought she was strong enough to stand.

How she envied Paul and Tammy their uncomplicated happiness. They loved each other, and there were no obstacles to their loving. Whereas she . . .

A desire for someone's arms to hold her and give her the safety she longed for was like a physical pain. No, she admitted to herself. Not *someone*'s arms. She drew in a shuddering breath that brought Daks's head to look into her face. Dan's arms. In spite of everything, she wanted him. And where was the sense in that? How could she be burning up with longing for comfort from the very man who was the cause of all her unhappiness?

Why couldn't love follow a sane pattern, growing only in people like Paul and Tammy, nice, suitable people? Why should it flower so hopelessly, so unfruitfully, so one-sidedly in herself? She thought of Alan, who would so contentedly settle for a much tamer kind of love. He, too, was destined for a measure of unhappiness. He would get over it, of course. His feelings were too firmly anchored in common sense for him to go on wanting someone like herself when it was obvious that she had nothing to offer him. How crazy, though, to think that she could possibly stay around in the middle of all this emotional chaos.

No. The only possible solution was for her to accept the agents' valuation of the Stables, and move somewhere far away where she could find fresh work and attempt to start again.

The workmen's noise seemed to have stopped. It was six o'clock, and Dan had either not chosen to come over and speak to her, or else he had not returned to the Dower House tonight. No doubt he would be back in whichever penthouse was convenient now that work had started here.

Ros got up and fetched her writing case. Dan would be back to see the workmen in the morning, if not tonight. And when he came, he would find her note telling him that he had won. She wasn't going to give herself the chance to change her mind. She was going to accept his offer, leave the Stables, leave Gateway, get out of his orbit. It was the only course of action that made sense.

She began to write.

CHAPTER NINE

A KIND of exhausted resignation filled Ros as she sealed the envelope and addressed it to Dan. She was aware of the fragility of her composure but, after the torment of not knowing what was going to happen, the very fact of having made up her mind was some sort of relief. Its anaesthetic effect on the pain she knew she ought to be feeling wouldn't last. She had to go through with delivering the letter quickly, now, before the numbness wore off.

Daks's ears drooped as he saw her take down his lead.

'Can't be helped, boy,' she told him. 'There's too much for you to interfere with over at the house now. I know you'd rather go free.'

Free. She wondered, as she clipped on his lead, how long it would be before she too felt free again. She could go through the motions of cutting loose, but severing mental and emotional ties was a different matter. Doing the sensible thing was relatively easy. Feeling sensible about it was something that might turn out to be very hard indeed.

As she came out of the courtyard, that point was instantly driven home. Dan was coming towards her. The moment she saw him, her fragile peace

was shattered, and she was prey to a hundred and
one conflicting emotions. First came an involuntary
thud and race of her heart at the sight of him, then
an overpowering urge to run away, and finally
contempt for herself, because the smile that broke
out on his face—even though one part of her was
hating him—seemed to tug at a need to respond
deep inside her.

The effort to control all these warring emotions
went on inside her. Her face was quite
expressionless as she held out the envelope to him.

'I was coming over to deliver this. You may as
well take it.'

He was looking closely at her, eyebrows raised,
quizzing her.

'What's this I see? The Frosted Blonde look back
again? I thought we'd seen the last of her.'

'Don't fool around, Dan,' she said coldly. 'Just
take this and go.'

He looked at the envelope but didn't take it. 'If
it's a complaint about the noise over at the house,
today was the worst, and it won't go on for ever.'

'I'm not complaining. Neither am I joking.'

His face was gradually losing the look of
amusement. 'So I see. Well—perhaps you could at
least tell me what's bugging you instead of all this
nonsense.' He waved aside the letter. 'You've got a
voice, haven't you? Come on, Ros. Speak. There's
plenty I want to say to you when you've got this
mood out of the way.' He thrust his hands in his
pockets and rocked impatiently as he challenged her.
'Are you angry I didn't tell you work was starting?

Is that it? I had every intention of coming over to speak to you tonight, well before I got your message—and I *have* had one or two other things to arrange in the course of my working day.'

'I'm sure you have,' she said cynically. 'Well, I can save a bit of your precious time. You don't need to tell me anything. I've seen it all. I've seen what you're preparing to do to the Dower House—and what you've already done to the summer-house.' For the first time her face reflected her feelings. 'You couldn't wait, could you?'

'As a matter of fact—no.' Something—it seemed like the shine of suppressed excitement was lurking at the back of his eyes. 'Before you start getting too worked up, though, there's something you ought to know.'

'If you're going to tell me about Gateway, you needn't. I know all about that, too. Alan told me.'

'Did he, damn it!' Dan frowned. 'I distinctly told him to keep his counsel until the thing was official. I hope he hasn't gone shouting it from the rooftops, or he'll find he's queered his pitch with the Education Office. I did, of course, intend telling you that tonight, too.'

'Don't blame Alan. It's his school, and as far as he's concerned you're some kind of saint. He was over the moon about it, and he thought I would already have some idea of what you intended. I believe he actually thinks we're friends.'

He was watching her with puzzled eyes now. 'And aren't we? I don't understand your reaction, Ros. Or lack of it. I thought you would be the one to be over the moon to have the future of your school taken care of.'

Ros looked contemptuously at him. 'Pleased enough to show my gratitude by bowing gracefully out of the property you want?'

He narrowed his eyes as he stared at her in silence. Eventually he said, 'Are you implying what I think you're implying?'

'I'm saying congratulations, Dan. You finally worked out the right kind of currency to pull off your deal. Money and property couldn't persuade me, but how could I resist security for the kids I work with? Do you know what gets me more than anything, though? Your damned certainty that you'd got the exchange rate right. You couldn't even wait to hear my reaction, could you? You got your men started the minute Alan said, "Yes, please". I suppose I can count myself lucky that you haven't sent them in to gut the Stables before I've moved out!'

He was rigid with angry reaction to her words. 'You can count yourself lucky that I'm not turning you upside-down and beating some sense into you. What does a man have to do to buy a little favour in your eyes?'

'*Buy! Buy! Buy!*' she flung at him. 'Is there nothing in the world that doesn't have a purchase price in your estimation?'

He shot out a hand and grabbed her arm. 'Talking to you is a waste of time. Come with me.'

For the first time, Daks growled deep in his throat.

'It's all right, Daks,' Dan said. 'This is the way civilised human beings talk to each other.' The dog wagged his tail uncertainly, then whined, not sure of himself.

Ros said, 'Let go of me!' as she tried to tug her arm away.

'I warn you, Ros, I'll pick you up and take you back to the Dower House by brute force if necessary. You've worked out by sheer supposition what kind of bargain I'm after. Now you can come with me and see it on paper.' His eyes were eagle-cold as he looked down at her, but the pulse in his neck betrayed the white-hot anger ripping through him.

'You don't have to demonstrate the brute force. I'm sure it matches the financial empire,' she said scathingly. 'I'll come and give you the satisfaction of spelling out to me exactly what I'm enabling you to do to my place. Just don't touch me.'

He mockingly indicated that she should go ahead of him. 'You'll be glad you saw reason. Some of the men are still there. They'd have enjoyed the spectacle of you slung over my shoulder.'

'I hope this satisfies you,' Ros said as she walked ahead of him, smarting with humiliation, but too keen to hang on to her dignity to scuffle with him.

'What would satisfy me right now, lady,' he said in a voice that make her quicken her pace, 'would make that hair of yours curl even more than it does. And probably do you a power of good,' he added.

They were still several yards from the Dower House when the cry rang out—an unmistakable cry of pain followed by anxious voices and hurrying footsteps. Daks barked and strained at the lead. Dan rushed past Ros and ran ahead through the gates, and though she could have seized the opportunity to slip back home, it was so obvious that something unpleasant had happened that the idea did not enter her head.

The older man to whom she had spoken earlier in the afternoon was kneeling down beside someone lying crumpled on the path, and another man was bending anxiously over them.

'What happened, John?' she heard Dan ask the foreman.

'Tile fell off the roof, Mr Maxton,' the older man said, looking up. 'Nobody's fault. Nobody up there. We must have dislodged it earlier on.'

'Never mind whose fault it is.' Dan knelt down and spoke to the injured man. 'Tom? Just lie still a moment. You can hear me all right?' The man groaned and murmured something unintelligible. 'Good man,' Dan said, then spoke over his shoulder to the watching workman. 'First-aid box from the lorry. Quick as you can.'

He was pulling a handkerchief from his breast pocket as he spoke, and as he moved Ros saw that an alarming quantity of blood was pumping down over the injured man's face from somewhere in his hair. Dan pressed the handkerchief to the wound, talking all the time. 'There we are. This'll stop the leakage, Tom. Nothing like heads for creating a colourful scene. They look far worse than they are, always.' His voice was calm and reassuring, the kind of voice you would like to hear if you were hurt and didn't know where you were or quite how bad it was.

Ros stood watching, somehow hypnotised by the scene, unable to do anything even if it had been necessary, because of the need to restrain Daks.

Dan took the first-aid box from the young man who had been to get it, gave him a quick second look and said quietly, 'Better go and sit down, Kevin.'

'Sorry, Mr Maxton,' the man said groggily, looking like death. 'I never could stand the——'

'Just go and sit down.' Dan effectively silenced what the white-faced Kevin had been going to say and turned back to the injured man. 'Right, Tom. We'll soon have you patched up and on your way to let the hospital have a look at you. Pass me one of those pressure pads, John, then the wide crêpe bandage.'

Talking quietly all the time, his hands moved steadily until the dressing was in place.

'Oh—look at your suit, Mr Maxton,' Tom said shakily as Dan and the foreman helped him to sit up.

'Cleaning will take care of that,' Dan said reassuringly. 'Now, just stay put while I move the car as close as possible, and we'll have you sitting comfortably in no time.'

He had completely forgotten her, Ros realised. The little drama seemed to have been tailor-made to emphasise what a trivial factor she was in Dan's busy life. He had so much to do, so many irons in so many fires, and he was so competent to deal with them all. She was turning to slip away when he saw her and called out.

'Ros—make Kevin a cup of tea, will you? See that

he doesn't drive that lorry off before he's good and fit. Lock the door when you've finished—and check the rest of the doors and windows.'

So I have my small uses after all, she told herself drily. He was instantly involved again in helping Tom to his feet, not even waiting for her to acknowledge his orders.

'Not your car as well, Mr Maxton,' the man was saying. 'I don't want to mess that up as well as your suit.'

'Shut up, Tom,' Dan said kindly. 'You don't think we're taking you to hospital in a ruddy great lorry, do you? There we are. Comfortable?' He turned to the foreman. 'You'll come along, John? If there's a lot of waiting around, you can help. Let his family know, for one thing.'

As the car passed Ros, Dan called through the window, 'And don't disappear into the far distance. I still want to talk to you. I don't know when, but I'll be back.' Then they were gone.

Ros went over to speak to Kevin, who was now looking less grey in the face.

'What a bloomin' idiot I am,' he said sheepishly. 'It's a good job it wasn't just John and me left here. I'd have been no good to them at all.'

'You can't help it. That sort of reaction to blood is something that hits people irrespective of sex or toughness. I'm going to make you a drink. Want to come inside?'

He shook his head. 'Better out in the fresh air.'

Ros went into the house alone and shut Daks in the cloakroom while she made tea in the kitchen.

The house was full of memories, and she would have preferred not to come in and see the furniture labelled as it was according to some disposal plan of Dan's. She steeled herself not to look closely, and tried to shut her mind to it and concentrate only on the simple task she was performing.

When the restored Kevin had driven off in the lorry, she went back inside for the last time to wash the mug and replace it in the kitchen. Then she released Daks, who had been whining anxiously from the cloakroom. She took the note from her pocket and left it on the hall table, where Dan would be sure to find it when he got back, hoping that once he had read that, and had seen in black and white that she wasn't going to stand in his way any longer, he would leave her alone.

She didn't go home straight away. She walked up the path to the river and let Daks run ahead off the leash and enjoy the smells of the waterside. He didn't go far away. He kept returning to look up into her face, seeming to sense that her heart wasn't as much in the walk as it usually was. She was thinking how much both of them would miss the luxury of having the river so near, and wondering where they would eventually find themselves. Alan would release her from the end of the term if he possibly could, so there was every chance that she wouldn't be seeing this autumn in the woods.

Back at the Stables, she went over to her workshop for a while and attempted to do some work, but her unhappiness conveyed itself through her fingers to the pots she made. None was quite right and, in the end, after several attempts she scrapped the lot and squeezed them down into a mass of clay again.

She hadn't eaten, and it was foolish not to. Back in the kitchen she put Tammy's peeled potatoes on to boil and got a chop and vegetables out of the fridge. The phone rang as she was about to put the chop under the grill.

'Ros?' It was Tammy. 'Are you all right?'

'Of course. Why shouldn't I be?' Her voice was a hundred times brighter than she felt.

'I don't know. I'm upstairs in the flat. Paul's gone down with Graham to look at some stuff that's just come in. I thought . . . oh, I don't know. I wish I knew what you were going to do. When we've gone, I mean.'

'Well, I've decided, so I can tell you. The time seems ripe for a move, so I'm going away.'

'You are? Where?'

Ros gave a helpless laugh that had no humour in it. 'Give me a chance to find out first.'

'Have we pushed you into it, then?'

'No, not really. Just finally tipped the scales that were already swinging that way.'

'Come on out and eat with us, *please*.' Tammy's voice was exerting all its persuasive force.

'I've just started cooking my meal. I'm all right, really, Tammy. I'd rather leave it for tonight.'

There was a short silence, then Tammy said with feeling, 'It's that damned man, isn't it?'

'In so far as he has the Dower House now, and he's the one wanting to change our little world, you could say so.'

'More than that. He's managed to upset you more than anyone else ever has. Don't try to tell me otherwise. Odd, that, because at one time I would have sworn that he liked you—in fact that you——'

Ros couldn't listen to any more. 'Tam—my chop's beginning to burn,' she lied hurriedly. 'I must go. Thanks for ringing. Enjoy your meal.'

In the end Daks had the lion's share of the food she cooked and Ros filled up on coffee, which slid past the lump in her throat more easily. She made a note to ring the solicitor in the morning, and drafted a letter of resignation to leave with Alan when she had talked with him.

She was drawing back the curtains so that the kitchen light would shine out into the courtyard for Paul and Tammy when she saw the bobbing circle of light from a torch approaching, and knew with a sinking heart that Dan was keeping his word—for what reason she couldn't imagine. He must have seen her letter now, unless he had come straight over instead of going into the house.

'It's me,' he called unnecessarily before she steeled herself to open the door.

'How is he?'

'Ten stitches, but no serious damage, they think. They're keeping him in overnight to make sure. We had to wait ages—people brought in from a motorway incident took priority, not surprisingly. Then John spent a long time tracking down Tom's wife. She'd gone out and nobody was sure where. After that I had to go back and change. Are you alone?'

'Yes.'

'Then may I come in?'

Ros hesitated. 'Is there any need? I see you found my letter.' It was in his hand. 'I imagine that settles anything you might want to say.'

'You imagine too much. Five minutes, Ros. I told you earlier on I wanted you to see something.'

'Come in, then, if you must,' she said reluctantly.

He followed her into the kitchen and put a roll of paper on the table as he sat down tiredly on the bench. 'What a night!' He pushed his fingers through his hair. 'Have you ever drunk any of that appalling stuff from the machines in Casualty? They call it coffee. They should be sued.'

'I suppose that means you'd like a real cup?' This was only going to prolong things, she told herself as she went over to the coffeemaker. But he looked tired; probably hadn't eaten since midday, if then. and he had looked after one of his workmen as though he really cared about him.

Dan poured milk into the coffee she gave him and took a long drink. 'That's good.' He pushed her letter across the table. 'Is this serious?'

'Absolutely.'

'May I ask why you're doing it?'

Ros swallowed. 'Maybe I've just seen sense at last. After all, this place is old and decrepit, as you said. The agents confirmed it. And I've just learned that Tammy and Paul are moving out. Maybe it seemed suddenly that it was the right time for me to go, after all.'

He folded his arms, looking hard at her. 'And

maybe you're lying your head off.'

She got up nervously. 'I didn't let you come in to conduct an interrogation. I can't pretend I'm altogether happy to leave, but that's my business. It's what you want. What more is there to say?'

He drained his coffee, still staring at her with those uncomfortable eyes. 'Is there something between you and that headmaster of yours? Is that why you've suddenly changed your mind?'

'I'm very fond of Alan.'

'Don't fob me off. Give me an honest answer.'

'What is it to do with you?' she said angrily.

'I've been studying you hard. Now you've suddenly jumped out of character. I want to know why. I know the man's keen on you. That stands out a mile. But what about you? Have I by any chance bought something I didn't anticipate—the chance for you and him to get together?'

Something in the way he asked—a genuine seriousness—made her give him a genuine answer.

'Alan would like that. But, as I said, I'm very fond of him. No more than that. I—shan't just be leaving here. I intend moving away altogether.'

'You mean you'd leave Gateway—after professing to value the school so highly?' he said incredulously.

'Someone will replace me. I'm not unique. And the main thing that concerned me was for the school to continue. That's going to be taken care of.' She looked pointedly at the clock. 'It's getting late, Dan. I really would like to call it a day.'

'And there's no other reason for your going

away?' His eyes were not leaving her face for a
second, and Ros wondered desperately how much
longer she could keep this up.

'Would you want to stay around with someone
who wanted to marry you, but whom you had no
intention of marrying?' She thought how ironic it
was that the reverse of that statement, concerning
not Alan but Dan himself, was even more true. Dan,
thank goodness, didn't know that. At least she was
spared that humiliation.

'Leave that, then.' But he hadn't finished.
'Earlier on,' he persisted, 'you began to say
something about my motives for supporting
Gateway. Would you like to explain a little?'

'What is there to explain? You know why you did
it.' Her eyes were not afraid to meet his now.

'I do. I'd like to know why *you* think I did it, apart
from obvious reasons like Gateway being an
excellent place, and the kids worth helping, and
Debra's chance of recovery worth celebrating.
Enough there to justify what I've done, I should
have thought.'

Ros faced him squarely. 'I think you did it for all
those reasons to some extent—I'll grant you that.
But I also think you had another, less worthy reason.
According to Alan, you more or less said as much.
What were your words? "A certain young lady's
gratitude will be my reward, I hope." Alan thought
you meant Debra. I think you meant me.'

He was honest enough not to deny it. 'A pretty
fair assessment of the situation.'

'And that was the form my gratitude was expected

to take.' Her finger shook as she pointed to her letter, and she quickly withdrew it and clasped her hands behind her back.

'Wrong!' Something seemed to have snapped in him. He had leapt up as he almost shouted the word, and he was striding to and fro, pacing the length of the kitchen like a caged tiger. 'How is it that a man who has established more than one successful business and found it comparatively simple, a man who has brought off more deals than he can count—and decidedly to his own advantage—how is it that that man can so mishandle dealings with one woman?'

'Mishandle? I think you judged the situation very successfully.' She turned round and leaned against the table, watching him. 'You've admitted as much. Now you can go ahead and build your precious leisure centre.'

He glared dementedly at her, his hair ruffled, his earlier calm vanished. 'That would be all very well—if I still intended the Dower House to become a hotel.'

Ros felt to be getting more and more enmeshed in something she couldn't understand; an *Alice Through the Looking Glass* conversation where nothing was as it seemed, nothing made sense.

'Have you been drinking?' she said suspiciously.

That made him hit the roof. 'There isn't a drink strong enough to make a man equal to dealing with a woman like you. You're a mass of prejudice. You're as obstinate as a thousand mules. You misinterpret everything I say to you.' He stopped

opposite her. 'I ought to thank the gods above that
there's a prospect of getting rid of you.' His hands
shot through his hair again, hovered over her
shoulders, twitched away. 'Oh—for goodness' sake,
sit down, will you? Since words go so far wrong, see
if something you can focus your eyes on gets through
to you.'

He waited impatiently until she had pulled out a
chair again and sat down. Then he unrolled the
papers he had brought and spread them out on the
table in front of her, breathing raggedly but saying
no more.

Ros realised slowly that she was looking at a plan
of the Dower House, practically unchanged. There
were no wings branching out across the lawn, just
the addition of a shaped terrace, labelled 'Cotswold
Stone', and a path of the same stone going
towards——'

'What's this?' She pointed unbelievingly to
something at the end of the path.

'You know perfectly well what it is. The summer-
house.'

'And these are your current plans?'

'They are.'

'But you've already started to destroy the
summer-house. I don't understand.'

He put a smaller paper down on top of the plan.
Headed 'Andrew Tidiman, Thatcher', it was a
quotation. 'To rethatching existing outbuilding . . .'
it read. The sum named represented several months'
salary to Ros, but so much more. She looked up at
him, not ashamed that her eyes were shining over

with tears. 'You're keeping it?'

'It seemed the thing to do.' He put another set of papers in front of her. Work sheets for repairs to the house. Relaying floors. Replastering walls. Repointing the external walls. The list went on, minute in detail.

She spoke with difficulty. 'I'm glad—so glad the Dower House will remain a home.' She swallowed hard. 'What about the Stables?'

'I imagined they'd stay pretty much as they are. A house for people to live in. Workshops.'

'But not me. I won't be there.'

'I never meant you to be.' It sounded so callous, so matter of fact. Ros jumped up and would have moved away, but he rose quickly with her, caught her hand and held it. 'Wait, Ros. I'm trying to spell it out as clearly as I can for you. It isn't easy for me. When you're a businessman dealing with a customer you know is going to be tricky, you don't put all your cards on the table at once. You try to win him round subtly, little by little. Convince him that you've got principles, that he'll get a satisfactory deal. That's the way I tend to go about everything. The habit sticks. Do you see?'

Ros looked from his hand gripping hers up to his face. She was beginning to imagine the most unbelievable things, and she dared not. She could be about to make the most incredible fool of herself.

'I'm not sure that you're making things any clearer at all,' she said shakily.

'Then here come the cards, face up on the table. Every one of them. You remember being surprised by the fact that I hadn't so far bothered to establish a permanent home of my own?'

His eyes were burning into hers and she nodded slowly. 'Yes, I remember.'

'Then you also remember the reason I gave you? That for me, the girl would come first. Once I'd found her, then I'd get myself a home. You remember that, Ros?'

This time, the nod she gave was scarcely perceptible. She had never felt herself so much on the edge of a precipice. Part of her thought she knew—incredibly, wonderfully—what he was leading up to. But she had jumped to so many wrong conclusions. Now she was terrified that he might still be going to tell her something she couldn't bear to hear.

It seemed for one awful second that her worst fears were realised when he said, 'Well, I was wrong, wasn't I?' But her heart thudded again as he went on to add, 'I found both the girl and the house together, didn't I? Tell me I did, Ros.'

She was bursting with such a tumult of feelings that she could hardly speak, but somehow she did.

'You know me. You said it yourself: I misinterpret everything that's said to me. Spell out a direct question, and I'll give you a straight answer.'

She thought she could see laughter dawning at the back of his eyes. 'The final card? All right, my demon bargainer. Can you bring yourself to marry a man who's the complete opposite of everything you thought you wanted?'

Excitement was bubbling up in Ros like champagne

bubbles in the blood, and yet she held back. 'You're still speaking in riddles.'

He gripped her shoulders, and half laughing, half deadly serious, said, 'Answer me, damn it! Will *you* marry *me*?'

Ros's answer was a strangled 'Ooh!' of mingled relief and joy as she flung herself at him and clung to him with all her strength.

Dan crushed her to him and kissed her with a hunger that matched her own. For a long moment they clung together, then he broke away to say huskily, 'You're forgetting something. You insisted on the question. Now I want my answer.'

Her face was flushed, her eyes luminous. 'I don't want to talk!' She was attempting to get close to him again, but he held her away with devilish strength.

'Ros?'

'Oh, yes! Yes—yes—yes—yes!' She punctuated the words with kisses and they clung together again, laughing as Daks leapt frantically at them from all sides, making them overbalance on to the settee that was so providentially out of place in the kitchen.

'Your dog is going to have to get used to this, or I'm going to be a very frustrated man,' Dan said, fighting off Daks's attempt to squeeze on to the settee between them.

Ros got up and took a few 'Good Boy' chocolates from the box on the windowsill and scattered them over the floor. Daks's attention was instantly one hundred per cent devoted to finding and eating them.

'We all have our priorities,' she said as she slipped

back into Dan's arms.

'Why did we waste so much time?' she asked him later, her head resting on his shoulder, his arm warm around her. 'How could I have thought a place was so important? When it came to the question of leaving, it wasn't this place I thought I'd never manage to live without. It was you.'

'Property never was the real issue between us. It was your gigantic objection to everything I stood for. You couldn't see me, only my background. I had to break through that somehow.' He rested his face on her shining hair. 'As for me—I knew from our second meeting, when you defied me in your own updated version of David and Goliath, that you were going to mean a whole lot of joy as well as a certain amount of trouble. You do realise,' he added seriously, turning her face up to his, 'that I'm not really changed at all? I'm still going to go on getting ideas and putting them into practice. Making money, inevitably. In fact, unless the bottom drops out of the market, it's difficult to see how I could *not* go on making money, even if I never had another idea in my life. But the world's idea of success would be empty without you, Ros. I want to be sure you understand that.'

'How could I not understand when you look at me like this?' she said softly, wondering how she could ever have thought his eyes inscrutable. They were warm, eloquent, speaking volumes to her.

'And you'll help me find other causes like Gateway to appease that vulnerable conscience of yours?' he said. 'That way we can both be happy, my little puritan.'

She paused, her lips tantalisingly close to his. 'But you, my darling Dan, are going to be proved oh, so wrong on one score.'

'And what's that?'

'The appropriateness of calling me your little puritan.'

She made sure that, even if he had intended answering, he had no chance to do so.

HARLEQUIN

Romance

Coming Next Month

#3043 MOUNTAIN LOVESONG Katherine Arthur
Lauren desperately needs help at her northern California holiday lodge, so
when John Smith, handyman *extraordinaire*, appears out of nowhere, he
seems the answer to her prayers. The only question—how long can she depend
on him?

#3044 SWEET ILLUSION Angela Carson
Dr. Luke Challoner, arrogant and domineering, expects everyone to bow to his
will. He is also one of the most attractive men Marion has ever met—which
doesn't stop her from standing up for herself against him!

#3045 HEART OF THE SUN Bethany Campbell
Kimberly came home to Eureka Springs to nurse a broken heart. Alec
Shaughnessy came to examine Ozark myth and folklore. Both become
entangled in a web of mystery that threatens to confirm an old prophesy—that
the women in Kimberly's family might never love happily.

#3046 THAT CERTAIN YEARNING Claudia Jameson
Diane's heart goes out to vulnerable young Kirsty, but warning bells sound
when she meets Kirsty's dynamic and outspoken uncle, Nik Channing. Yet she
has to support Kirsty, even if it means facing up to her feelings . . . and to Nik.

#3047 FULLY INVOLVED Rebecca Winters
Fight fire with fire—that was how Gina Lindsay planned to win back her ex-
husband. Captain Grady Simpson's career as a firefighter had destroyed his
marriage to Gina three years earlier. But now she's returned to Salt Lake
City—a firefighter, too. . . .

#3048 A SONG IN THE WILDERNESS Lee Stafford
Amber is horrified when noted journalist Lucas Tremayne becomes writer-
in-residence at the university where she is secretary to the dean. For Luke
had played an overwhelming part in her teenage past—one that Amber prefers
stay hidden. . . .

Available in April wherever paperback books are sold, or through
Harlequin Reader Service:

In the U.S.
901 Fuhrmann Blvd.
P.O. Box 1397
Buffalo, N.Y. 14240-1397

In Canada
P.O. Box 603
Fort Erie, Ontario
L2A 5X3

HARLEQUIN
American Romance®

Live the

Rocky ☆ Mountain Magic

Become a part of the magical events at The Stanley Hotel in the Colorado Rockies, and be sure to catch its final act in April 1990 with #337 RETURN TO SUMMER by Emma Merritt.

Three women friends touched by magic find love in a very special way, the way of enchantment. Hayley Austin was gifted with a magic apple that gave her three wishes in BEST WISHES (#329). Nicki Chandler was visited by psychic visions in SIGHT UNSEEN (#333). Now travel into the past with Kate Douglas as she meets her soul mate in RETURN TO SUMMER #337.

ROCKY MOUNTAIN MAGIC—All it takes is an open heart.